HIS TO TRAIN

Sons of Sicily - Book Two

SKYLAR WEST

Published by Blushing Books
An Imprint of
ABCD Graphics and Design, Inc.
A Virginia Corporation
977 Seminole Trail #233
Charlottesville, VA 22901

Skylar West
His to Train

eBook ISBN: 978-1-64563-974-9
Print ISBN: 978-1-64563-975-6
v1

Prologue

Dean presided over the backyard, watching his younger siblings play while the hot girl beside him fidgeted. He knew that Jimmy Falcone, Mag's father, wanted someone to protect his daughter and treat her like the princess she was. If he played his cards right, he would be that someone.

Dean's mother called in his brothers, leaving Maggie and Dean alone in the backyard. "Uh, is that a treehouse I spot through the branches?" Maggie was pointing to Dean's childhood hangout, his personal space that was only for him. His father had built another one for his brothers, leaving the tree penthouse for Dean alone.

"It is. Would you like to see it?"

Maggie's eyes had found his. She gulped as she said, "Yes, please."

Taking her hand, he led her to the treehouse. He was looking forward to having her in his space, where he had all the control. He sent her up first, in case she fell, so he could catch her. Maggie was two years younger and considerably smaller, while Dean was considered the school's hot jock and was built like a much older guy. Maggie, he determined, was too hot and too beautiful for a girl her age.

Dean wanted her, but not now. She was too young. He could wait, but he needed to let her know that she belonged to him. Once they were in the treehouse, they were entirely shaded by the extensive branches that had grown since the house was built.

"Wow, this is cool," Maggie commented as she wandered around the space looking at Dean's things.

He leaned back against the entrance wall, watching her. "Tell me, Maggie, about this MagsT entertainment. Are you branding already?"

Maggie had giggled. "My dad's girlfriend, who put the party on, did those for me. I've been banned from posting on social media for a while. But she did it under our two names, like a company, so he didn't get mad."

"Why were you banned from using social media?" Dean's eyes glinted with interest when Maggie's cheeks bloomed with color. "Nothing specific."

"You're lying, Maggie. Are you always that bad at it?"

Maggie's eyes went from being round in surprise to narrowing in annoyance in a nanosecond. "Maybe; it's hardly any of your business."

And there it was, that princess act she pulled when she was avoiding confrontation. She might get away with it with others, but she wouldn't with him.

"I think you need a lesson, Maggie, in how to treat others with respect." She spun on her heel, looking out the only window in the treehouse. Dean moved and stood behind her, so near there was no doubt Maggie could feel his breath on her ear. "You act like a spoiled princess when you want to avoid what makes you uncomfortable. That won't fly with me. Now, tell me what you did."

Maggie shrugged her shoulders like what she was about to

share was no big deal. "I made a friend online; his name was David. He was super cool, and we started chatting after I liked a bunch of his photos."

Dean tried not to tense, not wishing to give away how annoyed he was getting by the direction of Maggie's confession. "So, anyway, we decided to meet, and he no-showed. When my father found out I tried to meet up with a guy I didn't know, he set some restrictions in place regarding my Instagram use."

Dean knew there was more to the story. "I call bullshit! What are you leaving out?" Maggie tried to move, to get away from Dean. He could almost feel her squirming with her desire to run away. He wanted to laugh outright, but he held his laughter in place. "Come on, Mags, tell me."

"Fine," she sighed. "My dad's girlfriend Theresa is a blogger, and when I told her about David, she asked me to show her his account. When she saw it, she said it was fake and not to meet him. I told her off at the time, not believing her, but she said she would prove it to me. We set up a time to meet David at the track, and Theresa disguised herself as me.

"Thankfully, she'd alerted her best friend's husband, a detective, to what her plan was, and he came as back up, pretending to be a jogger. David never came. But a man in a van did, pretending to be David's father. He grabbed Theresa, trying to get her to his van, but she fought him off. It turns out that she was right. David wasn't real, and the guy they caught was a pedophile."

Dean boiled with rage. How stupid could she be? Who the hell tried to meet up with someone from the internet? "What was your punishment?"

Maggie blushed at Dean's question and glanced toward the treehouse's only exit.

Dean placed his hands gently on her shoulders.

"Well, I told you, he has put in social media restrictions, and I was grounded for a bit."

"That's it?" Dean asked, astounded. "It's no wonder you are such a brat. He should have spanked your ass black and blue."

Maggie whirled around and glared at Dean. "I am not a brat. I'm my dad's princess."

"Exactly," Dean glared back, "a brat."

"You, you, I hate you, Dean DeLuca. You are so mean!"

Dean couldn't hold back the chuckle as she stamped her foot down on the wooden floorboards. "You may hate me, princess, but one day you will bow at my feet, and if you're a good girl, I may reward you."

The shock of his words was evident on Maggie's very expressive face. But what was most apparent was that his words had spiked in her a curiosity he knew, one day, he would make good on.

"You wish," she said, repeating the stomp of her foot on the treehouse floor.

Dean's phone beeped with a message.

> *Mr. Falcone:* Can you keep her for dinner?
> *Dean:* Yes, sir.
> *Mr. Falcone:* I hope she's behaving herself.
> *Dean:* Yes, sir, it's educational.
> *Mr. Falcone:* Interesting response. See you soon.

"Was that my dad? Is he coming to get me out of here?"

"Not yet." Dean gazed down at her meaningfully. "You're staying for dinner, little brat."

Maggie didn't respond.

"Now, where were we? Oh yeah, you were throwing a fit. As I said, he should have tanned your behind."

Maggie attempted to leave the treehouse then, and Dean

was almost tempted to allow it. But then his rage at her stupidity came back, and he knew what he needed to do. After today, no matter what happened, she would be his. He then spanked Maggie hard on her shorty shorts-clad ass.

She screeched, spun around and glared at him. "Who the hell—"

"Now, now, princess, it was just a little spank. I think you should have another." Dean spun her around and laid down a hard one, and she squealed. "Remember this moment, Margaret Falcone, it is the one in which I marked you and made you mine."

Maggie ran out of the treehouse and down the ladder, with Dean following at a distance. He was giving her a chance to process what had just happened. When Dean went into the house, it was to find Maggie in the kitchen talking to his mom like they were old friends. He stood and watched until it was time to carry the dishes to the table.

Dean was almost embarrassed at the attention Maggie, the Falcone princess, was receiving from his father. No doubt he would try to twist this into something for his own gain. He loved his father, but the man was a total opportunist.

An hour later, the doorbell rang. Dean answered while Maggie put on her shoes and grabbed her bag.

As she passed by him, she hissed, "Let's not do this again."

Dean sniggered. "Don't forget, princess, one day you will be on your knees."

Maggie stuck out her tongue at Dean as she got in the car. His palm itched with the desire to spank her pert, insolent behind, and he couldn't wait for the day when Maggie Falcone found herself over his lap.

Chapter 1

Seven years later...

"**M**aggie!" Jimmy Falcone yelled from the bottom of the massive staircase in the Falcone mansion where Maggie had lived her entire life. Jimmy turned back to the man standing behind him, offering an apologetic smile.

"Sorry, Dean, you know what she's like."

"I do, Mister Falcone, but I don't mind. She's worth the wait." The older man's eyes narrowed at Dean. "Is she? Unlike T and I, who had to force our way out of my father's clutches, you two have been destined since the beginning, chosen to unite our two families."

"Yes, Mr. Falcone, I understand. But Maggie has been balking these plans since the beginning. We were close until I left high school, and I haven't been around much these past few years. Are you sure this is still the plan you want?"

Jimmy's gaze continued to pierce through Dean's armor. Could he see his barely disguised desperation to have Maggie all to himself?

"I have seen you two together; don't worry about it. Maggie will see the advantages of this marriage. Besides, you have both grown up over the years. I'm sure whatever petty issues Maggie had as a girl are long gone."

Yeah right. If only he knew, Dean thought.

"I'm going to go see what's taking her so long. I'll be right back. Take a seat; make yourself comfortable."

Dean sat on one of the many furniture pieces in the elaborate entryway and thought back to that day when his father had broken the news to him—he would be marrying the Falcone princess, Margaret.

His father and Jimmy had pulled him aside at graduation. The Falcone Family, who had become close friends with the DeLucas, had been there to cheer Dean on. Graduating with a football scholarship and being Valedictorian had been a big deal.

"Dean, Jimmy and I have been talking. We want to unite our two empires. When you are done with school, you're marrying Margaret Falcone and uniting our two families. We'll talk more later, but I wanted to give you fair warning, as Jimmy will announce it tonight at your celebration dinner."

Dean had been shocked. He'd wanted her ever since he'd seen her photos from her thirteenth birthday party on her Instagram profile. At school the next day, Dean talked to her for the first time about being invited to her next party. Then, her father had asked Dean to take Maggie home with him and keep watch over her. Dean had been more than happy to comply and have the sweet Maggie all to himself. Who would have known that day would create the camaraderie the two families now had.

Dean looked up as Maggie and Jimmy appeared at the top of the staircase. Dean had only seen pictures of Maggie via social media since he'd left school. She looked like her photos, but they didn't capture her sultry energy. She'd grown up since he saw her at her high school graduation. He'd teased her about his promise in the treehouse from when they first hung out together.

Dean had known long before that day what type of girl Maggie was and what kind of woman she would turn into. Now, he planned on fixing all the mistakes Jimmy had made with his daughter. She was so spoiled, and Dean needed to nip it in the bud now. If they were to walk down the aisle together in three months, contract or no, he wouldn't put up with her shenanigans.

Mags descended the stairs, wearing skin-tight jeans that showed off her delicious curves and long, slim legs. She wore a halter top and carried a jacket and her purse. When she saw Dean at the bottom of the stairs, her eyes narrowed with disdain.

"Luca, it's been a while."

Dean wasn't sure how he felt about her shortening his last name and calling him by it, but he smiled at her. Let her have this moment, for it would be the last one. "Princess Maggie, lovely to see you," Dean said, taking her hand and kissing the back of it. She didn't respond, just watched him with distrust in her eyes. Dean would enjoy their evening out, the first of many to come.

"Mr. Falcone."

"Please, Dean, stop being so formal. Jimmy, please."

"All right, Jimmy. I have booked a weekend away for the lovely bride-to-be and myself. I hope that isn't an issue?"

Jimmy smiled broadly. "Not in the least. I hope you two have some quality time. Speaking of, I promised my wife some help with the twins. They are a handful. Have fun, you two."

Jimmy left Dean and Maggie alone as he raced up the stairs and out of view.

"Let's go, princess, your chariot awaits." Dean escorted Maggie to the car, opening the door for her and ensuring she was tightly secured in the seat belt. She glared at him but said nothing.

When he got in his seat and pulled out onto the street, she found her voice. "So, where are we going?"

"Geno's, of course."

"Seriously, cheesesteak corner? I should have known."

"What should you have known, princess?"

"That you would take me somewhere lacking in hygiene. Seriously, we're going to sit out at one of those disgusting tables to eat dinner?"

Dean smiled at her outburst. "No, we weren't. We were going to pick it up and take it elsewhere. Keep it up, princess, and you won't be eating at all."

Dean inwardly chuckled at Maggie as she attempted to stamp her foot in the car, but it was difficult, being secured in and wearing tight pants. Instead, she sat forward and slammed herself back into her seat, glaring at Dean. He couldn't help it; he broke down into laughter at her antics while her temper sparked out of control. She slapped Dean hard across the face. When he turned toward her, she had the sense to shrink back into her seat.

"Now that dinner is off, I will take you to our second location."

Maggie quieted and made no physical outbursts of temper, no doubt wondering what was going to happen. The short drive to Old City was spent in silence. When they arrived on Arch Street and pulled up to a large brownstone, Maggie looked quizzically at Dean.

After helping her from the car, Dean led her around back to the private garden. It was packed and lush, and the outdoor lights were on.

"Where are we, Dean? What is this place?" At least she was using his correct name.

"I have something to show you, this way." Dean led Maggie over to the corner to a massive tree with a sturdy ladder going up into the canopy. "You first, princess." He followed behind, enjoying the view of the wagging, luscious ass that was a few feet above him.

When they got to the top, they stepped into Dean's treehouse, the one from his backyard. Jimmy and Dean's brothers had helped to disassemble and put it back together with a few added updates. "No way. Is this the same treehouse?"

"It is. I wanted it here. I wanted our first moment together to be immortalized. Your father and my brothers helped me move it here. I had to find the perfect tree first, which led to the hunt for the perfect house. Welcome, Maggie, to your future home."

She smiled for the first time that evening. "This is pretty cool. It would have been better with dinner, though." She was no longer looking at him but gazing around like she had the first time, seven years earlier. "I'm sorry about earlier."

"You mean slapping me across the face while I was driving? You aren't sorry, but you will be."

Now her eyes flashed at Dean. "I don't understand."

"I know, but you will, and you will also remember the promise I made you." Maggie's cheeks flushed a lovely pink, highlighted from the many twinkling lights that were strung. "Now, the question is whether you'd like your spanking in the treehouse, where all your new neighbors will hear if they are outside, or would you like it in your soundproofed home?"

"Soundproofed?"

"Oh yes, Maggie, it is soundproofed for many reasons. Mostly, so when you scream out my name when I make you orgasm, the neighbors don't call the cops."

She opened and closed her mouth several times, formulating words and then changing her mind.

"Now, what will it be?"

"Neither; I won't let you spank me, DeLuca." She made her decision by calling him by his last name, and Dean had made his.

Grabbing her by the elbow, he moved over to the bench he'd made just for this purpose. He sat down and pulled a kicking Maggie over his lap.

"Don't you dare, you, you heathen," she spat out.

He swung his leg over hers and yanked her jeans down over her hips. Maggie squealed in protest as Dean's hand came down hard on her virgin backside. The air rushed out of her lungs as she wiggled and fought to get free.

"Now, little principessa," *smack, smack, smack*, "let's go over why you're here." Before Dean could continue, his naughty princess attempted to bite his calf. "Oh, so feisty. Good, I like my women to be strong." *Smack, smack, smack!* He continued to rain down his hand on her unprotected backside.

Dean had been preparing for this moment for months and knew exactly how it would play out. He wrapped his hand through her hair, drawing her up to her feet. "Now, little brat. You will go stand in that corner and think about your behavior."

"No."

Dean's smile appeared feral, and he saw the hesitation in Maggie's eyes when she wondered at the logic of her reaction. Dean wanted her to know that anything but what he desired would be the wrong answer. So, grabbing one of the many implements he had placed inside the bench, he drew out a thick paddle and held it up for Maggie to see.

Her eyes grew round as he showed her the implement. With her jeans around her ankles, Maggie's attempt at escape with her limited gait had her tripping. Thankfully, Dean caught her before she hit the treehouse floor.

His face only inches from hers, he could see the fear in her eyes. For now, that would serve a purpose, but he didn't want fear in his wife-to-be, only obedience when he requested it. "Stand in the corner like a good girl, and I will only give you ten. You deserve more, and you know it, or you wouldn't be trying to run away."

Maggie gulped and studied his face while Dean did his best to look serious but not dangerous—that face he reserved for the assholes his family did business with. She nodded her consent, but that was not enough. She needed to say it.

"Maggie, you need to acknowledge my request with words. Say yes, sir."

But Maggie hesitated. "Last chance or you will receive fifty."

"Yes, sir."

"Good answer, now go and stand in the corner." He helped her shuffle to the corner, where he showed her where to put her nose and hands. Then he grabbed her hips and jutted her ass so he could admire the lovely shade of pink highlighted in the lights of the treehouse.

After waiting a few minutes, he called her back. "Margaret Falcone, please come back and drape yourself over the bench." As Maggie turned away from the corner she'd been standing in, Dean spotted the turmoil in her beautiful almond eyes before she shuttered them from him.

She shuffled toward him and looked up with begging eyes.

"Over the bench, stretch out your arms and grip the end, and stay in place."

Sighing, Maggie did as he asked, and as Dean stood waiting, she positioned herself just as he'd asked.

When he brought the paddle down on her backside for the first stroke, she let out a screech, like a banshee, and Dean smiled, glad she couldn't see his face. He gave her a moment to process the intensity of the sting. Then he brought the paddle down on her other cheek, and again, she squealed while he reveled at the livid red mark on her backside.

The next one covered both cheeks and had the desired effect, with Maggie sobbing but staying in place. Dean delivered the next five in quick succession, saving the last two for her tender sit spot. When he gave the first of the two, Maggie kicked her legs and wiggled in an apparent attempt to rid herself of the sting.

He delivered the last, then examining his artwork, Dean knew that all evidence of her spanking would be gone by the morning. The spanking had been intended to set the stage for tonight and their relationship in general. He wanted her to know what would happen if she mistreated him, and now that he had, he wanted to let her know what she would get when she obeyed him.

Dean sat down, pulling Maggie's hips onto his lap. He ran a finger down her entrance and found she was soaking. She had hated her punishment, but it had also excited her. Dean's cock stirred at this, as he'd hoped they would have this in common.

As her ran his finger lightly up and down Maggie's seam, she let out a low moan. Dean increased the pressure and gently pressed against her hardened nub, hiding just inside her wet folds. Maggie mewled and arched her back.

Dean grinned as he gripped one of Maggie's warm cheeks and delved a finger inside her with his other hand. He began with gentle pumps that increased with speed and impact as she wiggled and moaned her way toward her first orgasm.

But he wanted to see her face and watch the magic unfold as he brought her untold pleasure, so he lifted Maggie off his lap and laid her on her back. He parted her legs and leaned down, licking her seam from her gloriously hardened nub to her anus.

He continued to lick and nibble as Maggie moaned and thrust her hips. Dean inserted two fingers and began to hit Maggie's G-spot as he flicked her nub with his tongue. "Don't come undone until you ask permission, Maggie." It was cruel, he knew, but he needed to know that she would listen and obey his requests. This dynamic was critical to keeping her safe.

"Huh? What do you mean?" She stopped writhing, leaning up on her elbows to see his face.

"I mean, naughty girl, that if you want to have an orgasm, you have to ask permission." Not waiting for her to argue with him, Dean leaned back down and continued delivering the sensations he knew she was craving.

Maggie stayed on her elbows, watching him, her dilated pupils showing her pleasure. He watched the rapid rise and fall of her chest as her breathing became like a sprinter. He knew she was close, and continuing to fuck her with his hand, he said, "Don't forget to ask, Maggie."

"Yes, sir," came out in a breathy husk that increased Dean's hard-on painfully in his pants. He could feel her tightening, coiling, as her body moved closer to the ultimate release. And just when he thought she would disobey him, she screamed out his name, "Dean, please may I?" How could he say no?

"Now!" he commanded, and Maggie came apart, her sweet essence gushing over his tongue. Dean didn't want it to stop there, so he kept up the pace, and Maggie's body responded, tightening again as she rode the wave toward her next climax.

"Please, Dean, may I come?" Dean almost came undone this time when he gave her permission to release. She was so hot and wet, and all he wanted to do was bury himself deep within her. As her body quivered and calmed, she looked at him. "I need you inside me, Dean, please."

That was all the invitation he needed, and he stripped out of his clothing in record time. Dean lined himself up and entered her hot, tight channel. Finding a rhythm, he rode her, and when he felt her tighten and coil beneath him, he again pressed his thumb down on her nub, and she exploded around his cock.

He wasn't angry that she didn't ask permission as he hadn't asked her to during their lovemaking. The training, for the moment, was over, and now the pair was free to explore each other. Maggie reached up and ran her hand over his hard chest and gently thumbed his nipple. He, in turn, did the same to her, then dropping his head, he hungrily suckled her nipples while his pace intensified.

Maggie was writhing and moaning beneath him and greedily took all he gave her. He changed his angle and hit her G-spot hard, and she tipped over the edge again, crying out his name as she did so. Dean couldn't hold back and spilled into her convulsing channel.

Through their lovemaking, Maggie's pouty lips had been parted, creating the perfect O shape when she unleashed. Her eyes had looked at him with unabashed adoration as he wrung orgasm after orgasm from her gorgeous body. She was everything Dean had been dreaming of and more these past seven years.

He gripped her behind, and she let out a little yelp as she grinned up at him.

Dean smiled at her. "Hello, gorgeous, how are you?"

Her smile deepened. "I'm perfect, that was… something," she finished awkwardly.

"It was. Would you like to go inside and get cleaned up then see your new palace, princess?"

She nodded.

"Don't move, Mags. I have a supply of towels here for just such an occasion." She giggled, and the sound was like music to his ears, filling him with an unexpected lightness. When he came over to her with the small towel, he reverently cleaned her up and helped her to stand. Then he helped her get her panties and jeans on and had her sit down while he put her shoes on. All the while, Maggie watched him with a small happy smile curving her lips.

Chapter 2

Maggie had been nervous and had taken the upper hand as she'd descended the stairs, to keep Dean from seeing her knees knocking. When she first noticed Dean DeLuca in school, she'd fallen hard. He was gorgeous and popular and good at everything, just like she'd known her dad had been. Her stepmother and confidant Theresa had told Maggie many stories about her father when the two of them had been in school. Theresa had said that her father, Jimmy Falcone, had made many enemies, but the girls had loved him.

He oozed confidence and was good at everything, especially football. When Maggie watched Dean play football, she knew she'd found a guy as wonderful as her father. At least she'd hoped so.

After months of ogling Dean, he finally spoke to her after her thirteenth birthday. Theresa had helped her post pictures from the party, in which she'd looked seventeen. Dean had noticed her and happened to be with her when she received a very odd phone call from her father asking her to seek shelter with a friend, but not her bestie, Emma.

Her father asked to speak to Dean, and she had handed him the phone with an apologetic look, thinking that he would judge her and then despise her. She was surprised when he gave her back her phone and told her she was coming home with him.

She walked the six blocks to Dean's house with him, mostly in awkward silence. He emanated confidence and power just like her dad, and although she knew it was what she wanted, she was also terrified.

Did she want to fall in love with a dominant, confidant guy? It would help hide her faults if the attention was on him whenever they were together. But Maggie was not an introvert like his dad's bride. She was powerful and needed to be able to exercise it. Maggie had the ability to lord it over her peers, and she liked having the control.

But sometimes, she didn't want to. Occasionally, Maggie just wanted to disappear, and what could be better than to disappear into the presence of another strong personality, like Dean? After he called her a spoiled princess and landed a couple of smacks on her backside, she made it her mission to give him a hard time and never relinquish her power to him in any capacity.

Then their fathers had decided their future and announced it at Dean's graduation. Maggie would never forget the look on his face when the news was announced at dinner that evening. He meant to possess her, to own her, and did nothing to disguise how much he would enjoy it. Maggie had been dreading the day when she would be forced to deal with Dean DeLuca. As she descended the stairs, knowing tonight was the night, she put on her resting bitch face, deciding to make him work for everything, even common courtesy.

When he'd buckled her into her seat in his sports car, she'd gotten a whiff of his scent. She'd almost moaned out loud and had to dig her nails into her palm to stay silent. His masculinity was overpowering, and Maggie didn't know how long she could keep up her facade. The truth was she was very attracted to him, wanted him. But she didn't want him to know it.

When they left the backyard and moved around to the front to enter the house, Dean unlocked the door and then scooped her up. "What are you doing?"

"It's tradition to carry the bride across the threshold of her new home."

Maggie giggled and then said, "But we're not married yet."

Dean shrugged. "That's okay. I can't wait, and as we had sex already, I don't see us as being a traditional couple."

Once they were in the house, Dean placed her down on her feet like she was made of glass. Taking her hand, he led her around the brownstone.

"Holy crap, this place is way bigger than I could have guessed and, surprisingly, exactly what I would have chosen." Dean led her over to a state-of-the-art kitchen that included bar seating for six. "Wait, did my dad build this?"

Dean grinned. "He did, and Bobby decorated it for us."

"That explains so much, as my dad is a gourmet cook and would want me to have the same quality equipment." The work was top-notch, and every single square foot was custom. It would have cost a cool five million if the Family hadn't been involved.

The house was a fantastic blend of high-end entertainment and Family hominess. She was in awe at everything she saw, falling head over heels in love with the place. "How many bathrooms am I going to get stuck cleaning?" She was joking but not really. What would be the expectation of her in their domestic bliss? She was still pursuing what she wanted to be and do as a career. Would all of that end now? Would he want babies right away? Maggie felt stupid now for neglecting Dean the past few years and not giving them time to learn about each other.

"Don't fret, Maggie, we have years to have babies and can wait as long as you wish."

"How did you know what I was thinking?"

"Because I know you as well as I know myself. Every little frown spot means something different. Learning when they apply only to thoughts of you and when they apply to thoughts of us is very evident."

"It is?" she squeaked. "Sorry for being so predictable."

Dean smiled as he pulled her to his chest and gazed intently into her eyes. "Don't be sorry. And you are not so obvious to others, just to me, as it should be, Tesoro."

She could feel his hard-on pressing against her. She opened herself now, not holding anything back in her expression. "What am I thinking now, Dean?"

His grin was so dominantly sexual that Maggie felt her knees weaken. He held her upright, his face only inches from hers now. "You want me to take you to our new room and fuck you until you forget about everything. Now that you have been taken by me, you want it, and badly."

Damn him. How did he know how to read her so clearly? And then their conversation from seven years prior invaded her thoughts. He'd made sure she would want him, so she would crawl to him just like he threatened all those years ago.

His eyes darkened as he watched her.

"You made this happen. You have been planning everything, haven't you, Dean." She said it like a statement, not a question, and she'd hit the mark.

"Of course, I have. I don't take our relationship lightly or for granted. He gave her a meaningful look that had Maggie wanting to escape from his clutches. "No, princess, no more running. I gave you a taste in the treehouse of what you can expect if you disobey me. I ask nothing of you, Maggie, other than your obedience. You know what can happen if you don't. It can be a cruel world in the mafia, and now that you belong to me, it is my job to keep you safe. So, I will be very specific. You are free to do whatever you wish, whenever you wish, as long as I always know where you are, and if I ask something of you, you comply."

That seemed fair; after all, if she asked him something, she would expect the same. "I'll agree to your conditions as long as you agree to one of mine."

He looked as if he would say something, but he held his tongue and gave her a curt nod instead.

"I want the same courtesy. I want to know where you are, and when I tell you I need you, I want you to honor that."

Dean regarded her with an unreadable look. "I will agree to part of what you ask, as it is my job to keep you safe and not the other way around. I will not be keeping you abreast of my whereabouts at all times. But I promise you that every day of your life, I will be there for you, Maggie, and will check in with you. I will always be where you need me most."

"Then I accept your conditions."

"Excellent," Dean stated as he swept Maggie up in his arms.

Giggling, she asked where he was taking her.

"To take care of *your needs,* of course." Dean walked up to the third level, to the master suite, but Maggie didn't have time to observe the room and its beautiful décor.

Dean stood before her and fully undressed, allowing her time to peruse his body… and what a body! As a gifted football player, Dean had played since the age of seven and worked out with weights since twelve. He was big and muscular, with a tapered waist that led down to powerful hips and thighs.

His package was standing at attention, giving Maggie an eyeful of what had filled her so completely. What a magnificent cock, thick and long and perfect. Maggie licked her lips as she looked at Dean's manhood, desiring to feel it in her mouth. She slid down to her knees and flicked the tip.

She was thankful he hadn't brought up that she wasn't a virgin. She didn't know how she would share the story of her BOB romance. Her battery-operated boyfriend had brought her to so many climaxes since she hit fifteen years old. She wanted to be knowledgeable her first time, to be powerful. She may not have been with a man, but she had definitely practiced how to lick and suckle and although her vibrator had given her no feedback, Dean was now, as she continued to explore his cock. She took his length in her hand and gently squeezed. He was thicker and longer than her toy. She remembered the day she purchased it, blushing as she and T had looked at the selection online before ordering.

She wrapped her lips around the head as she began to gently pump his cock with her hand. Dean's head rolled back, and he emitted a guttural groan. She liked the reactions she was provoking, and feeling empowered, she lowered her mouth, taking his member to the edge of her throat.

Dean lowered to the bed and took her hair in his hand, fisting it and moving her now at the depth and pace he liked, showing her how to please him. In all of her playing, there had never been another person to grip her hair in this way. She found his control over her movements shockingly exhilarating.

There was freedom in being with someone willing to share exactly what he wanted and how to achieve it. Maggie moaned as he inched deeper, creating a vibration in his cock that even she could feel in her cheeks.

Maggie was curious. Did the moaning act like a vibrator, sending gentle tremors through his cock? She did it again, intentionally this time and louder. She felt the pressure tickle her lips as she did it.

"Just like that, principessa, you are doing wonderfully."

Maggie shuffled on the floor, trying to change her position and accommodate her knees when she suddenly found herself on the bed with her jeans ripped off. Dean moved her to her knees and pressed her chest into the bed. Then a smack rang out as he spanked her sore behind. She squealed, but before she could protest, he filled her with his hard length and all thoughts of protest were ripped from her as she processed these new sensations that being on her knees provided. Maggie wondered, as she was nearing her first climax, if she needed to ask permission.

"No, only when I tell you in advance. However," Dean continued, reading her mind again, "I may tell you to orgasm for me. I will train you to release and when to hold back. Now, my pretty mariposa, are you ready?"

"Yes."

"Yes, what?"

"Yes, sir."

"Good girl, now, release!"

And she did. Maggie came apart with the sensations Dean was delivering. He spanked her again as he continued to pummel her insides most delightfully. "Oh god, oh… my… goodness… Dean!" she screeched as a particularly intense wave overcame her, and she crashed, adrift in a sea of pleasure.

Dean groaned loudly as he spilled inside her quivering channel. When he was done, he went to the ensuite and retrieved a warm, wet cloth to clean her and patted her down gently with a dry one. Maggie felt completely satiated and well taken care of.

Dean joined her on the bed. Grabbing a remote from his nightstand, he pressed a button, and a wall fireplace lit up their space, allowing Maggie to peruse her new bedroom. The beach theme colors were so in contrast to her father's dark mahogany interior that Maggie found herself delighting in the trendy color palette.

"Uh, Dean, how do you know so much about my tastes? I mean, we haven't really seen much of each other in the past three years."

Dean's muscular arm was wrapped around Maggie, and he squeezed her a bit when he asked if she really wanted to know. "Instagram."

"What?" Maggie turned toward him in shock. "Surely, you are kidding?"

Dean laughed at her surprise. "No, and that leads me to my next topic. Instagram, you need to stop posting personal pictures."

Now Maggie was outraged. "What do you mean, stop? I am in fashion design school, Dean. Why would I stop? I need to be noticed."

Dean swung her around so she was sitting on his hips and would have no other choice but to look at him while they *talked*. "Really? So, you think you will get famous because of selfies on your personal profile? Sometimes you are so ignorant, Mags. Your father has done you no favors in allowing your behavior all these years."

Maggie was enraged and reached out to slap Dean's face, but he caught her wrist. "Not this time, princess. Now listen to me for a moment without trying to hit me, and I may let you off with a hand spanking. Pull that again, and you will be getting that new bath brush that is hanging in the shower."

Knowing he wasn't joking around, Maggie held still, and Dean let go of her hands. "Let me ask you this. Theresa, how many followers does she have?"

"About a million, and that is my point, Dean. I need to be visual to gain a following."

"Hold on a moment. Did Theresa publish personal photos of herself to build her blog business?"

"Well, no, I guess not."

"Exactly, and when I talked to her and your father, they both said that having anonymity helped propel Theresa forward and allowed them to lead a regular life."

"You asked them?"

"Of course, I did, and I also had someone run your profile to see how many of your ten thousand followers are into fashion. Guess what, none, zero, zip. What they are interested in is hot young women in barely-there clothing."

"Oh! Are you sure? That seems kinda crazy."

"No, what's crazy is all those shit heads from school getting to see pictures of your body ten times per day. That's crazy, and it's going to stop. Do you remember the Instagram pedophile who was caught after he tried to meet up with you?"

Now Maggie was growing uncomfortable and wondering if she could run and hide in the bathroom. "If you need to pee that bad, Mags, then pee here, but I'm not letting you go until we are done with this topic and you understand the gravity of what you have created."

She hated him pulling the upper hand with her, like he had so many times in high school. She found the intensity left her feeling unsure and childish. But he'd always been right, and he'd helped her navigate some intense situations that she would have preferred to flee from instead.

"That pedophile has been linked to the disappearance of twenty kids, a few of whom they found dead and buried in his back yard. He had pictures of Theresa from when she was around fifteen and wanted to get together with her. Unlike you, she didn't have anyone watching her back, and she went to meet the guy she thought was David. Thank god she hid in the bushes to see if the right person showed up."

Maggie gulped at the seriousness of what Dean was sharing. "I was so angry at you back then, Mags, for daring to meet up with an online crush. That day in the treehouse,

I promised myself that one day you would be mine, and when you were, I would keep you safe, even if it is from yourself."

Maggie felt tears building in her eyes, and unable to stop them, they slid down her cheeks.

"Do you see now why I want you to take down your personal account? But don't worry, I have a branding friend who is going to help you define and design your business page, okay?"

Maggie felt overwhelmed. Theresa had tried so many times to explain the same thing without being so blunt, and she'd never received the message, at least not like this. Dean had hit her somewhere vulnerable, and she didn't have words to explain her emotions.

"It's shame you're feeling at seeing the truth. It's like unveiling the eyes and gaining new sight," Dean said with genuine warmth and concern etched on his face.

"I don't know how you do that," Maggie finally got out. "I feel so lost right now, and I don't know you as well as you know me."

"You do, Maggie, you just don't realize it yet. And that's okay, you will, and you will learn why we work so well together when you stop fighting me on everything."

As Dean's words struck her, Maggie realized that she had been acting like a horrible brat, and that wasn't who she was. She bent forward and laid her head on Dean's chest.

He wrapped his strong arms around her while the tears fell silently, wetting his skin. When they stopped falling, Maggie felt renewed, like somehow the act had cleansed her soul.

"Are you feeling better?"

Maggie nodded and then remembered that Dean required words from her. "Yes, thank you. But I am rather hungry. Do you think we could get takeout, sir?" She knew the sir wasn't necessary in this case, but she also knew it would sweeten him up. And sure enough, she felt his cock harden beneath her belly.

"I can do better than that. Why don't you have a shower and dress and come into the kitchen when you're ready? Oh, and if you want to change into something more comfortable, you will find a basic wardrobe in your walk-in on the left."

Maggie was excited to try out her new bathroom and see what clothing Dean had chosen for her. She entered the massive bathroom and turned on the water in the shower. Figuring out how to turn on all six streams took her a minute, and then she relaxed, allowing the water to soothe her muscles.

She thought back to the beginning days of her dad and Theresa. Looking back with adult eyes, she saw things for what they were. Theresa had been a little broken, and through girl talk over the years, Theresa had explained what life had been like with Jimmy in the picture in her youth and then the hell it had turned into when James Sr. had moved them away. It was the first and only time Maggie had been angry with her grandfather, whom she adored.

As she dried off and went looking for her new wardrobe, Maggie thought back to when Dean had graduated. That was when things had shifted for her, and she became the ice queen. Until he left, he'd had her back. She hadn't seen that at the time, but she saw how profoundly he'd kept watch over her, upon reflection. Once he left, keeping up her frosty image had helped keep guys at bay and people from seeing the scared little girl inside.

Dean had undraped her frosty covering in one evening. It was good to have him back in her life if she was honest with herself. Maggie opened the sliding barn door to her closet to reveal a lot more than the basics. She beelined straight for the drawers and found bamboo lounging pants and a matching camisole. Getting dressed and looking in the floor-length mirror. Maggie liked what she saw. The clothing was so comfortable, she felt she was wearing pajamas, but she looked hot and sultry. Dean, she decided, had good taste.

She closed the closet and wandered back to the kitchen, where she found that Dean, dressed in only his pants, was busy cooking. Her breath hitched as she watched the gorgeous Italian man move around the kitchen like a pro. She could get used to seeing this daily.

When he turned and saw Maggie watching him, he grinned at her. "Sit, princess. I have a pillow there on that stool in case your ass is still sore."

Maggie blushed and tried a stool without a pillow. Discovering that her ass was still throbbing, she opted for the padded seat.

Once she was comfortably seated, Dean placed a plate of salad and steamed salmon in caper sauce down in front of her. It was one of her favorite meals. She was about to ask how and then remembered Instagram. She'd posted all of her favorite meals on there. They ate in companionable silence until it was time to clean up. Maggie stood up to remove their plates, but Dean told her to relax. He cleared, rinsed, and put their dishes in the dishwasher.

"Do you want to go home tonight, or do you want to stay here?"

That was a good question. What did she want? The idea of waking up in Dean's arms appealed to her, but the idea of being alone to process was also appealing.

She weighed out the pros and cons when Dean spoke up again. "I think you need some time to process your new reality. I'll take you home and then pick you up tomorrow afternoon for our weekend."

"Okay, Dean, that sounds good. Where are we going, by the way?"

"Camping."

Maggie turned large, surprised eyes on Dean. "Seriously?"

"No."

"No?"

"I was totally bullshitting. We are going to be here all weekend, getting to know each other better."

"You mean you are giving me time to catch up." Maggie laughed.

"That, and I want to hear about your last two years of high school. Your posts change at that time, and I think I need to know more about what went on."

Maggie was glad now that she was going home for the night. She had to think about how to talk about those two years as she wasn't proud of her behavior or the changes, and the last thing she wanted was a spanking for lying. She just needed time to strategize.

"Okay, but you have to fess up too. I feel like I am at a great disadvantage."

"That's how I like you, Maggie, at a disadvantage, but I'll answer any questions you have."

After he cleaned up the kitchen, Dean drove Maggie home and waited for her to enter the front door. When she waved goodnight, he left, and she entered her home with a sigh. What a night!

Chapter 3

Dean drove home to his temporary rental, where he'd been staying the past few months. Only his family and Jimmy had known he was back in town, as he wanted everything in place for tonight, and it had gone off even better than expected.

In the end, he'd decided that taking Maggie home was the best course of action. He had meetings the next day with the Marino Crime Family who had purchased Jimmy's empire. The daughter, Felicia, had been running things while her murderer brother Joseph had been sent back to Italy after kidnapping Theresa.

Felicia ran a tight ship, and her number two these past years had been Al, a man who had worked for Jimmy and whose father had worked for James Sr.. His daughter Emma was Maggie's best friend. They had been separated by the parents when Jimmy found out that Al had helped the Marino Family with Theresa's abduction.

And although Jimmy didn't press charges against Al, in fact, he kept him entirely out of the narrative for old times' sake, he'd still kicked Al out of the organization. Jimmy went straight and started off with his small company working on building homes in needier communities, under a contract with the government to better the failing neighborhoods. Bobby, Theresa's best friend, had been brought on as a head designer.

Bobby and Jimmy's success was legendary, their work moving into bigger and better things over the past seven years. Both now millionaires, they were the same guys they were when Dean had met them at age fifteen. One would think that type of success would have made one or both of them greedy and arrogant.

Dean noticed right away that he and Jimmy had things in common beyond Maggie. Both men enjoyed the spotlight, and navigating people was a breeze. Both had played high school and college football, and they were of similar build, tall and muscular. Jimmy still played ball with his old college buddies on Sundays, and Dean was invited to join them. This Sunday, Maggie would come with him and watch.

She'd attended all of her father's Sunday games until she was old enough to stay home alone. That was when the trouble started with her internet relationships. But that wasn't all that was going on for her at that time. Her grandmother, Maria, who had raised her, had passed away, leaving a floundering family of three behind.

Theresa attended the funeral service, which was how she connected with Jimmy, her childhood bestie. They had been neighbors for all of Theresa's childhood, and if you asked her, every good memory she had included bigger-than-life Jimmy Falcone.

Even after almost eight years together, they still behaved like newlyweds. They were lucky, for few couples had that type of love. Dean felt that he and Maggie would follow in their footsteps. He'd explained that by spanking Maggie in his tree-house when she was thirteen years old, he'd marked her as his.

When he thought about the promise to Maggie seven years

ago, the irony was apparent to him. He'd made the promise to her that she would one day be his, and it was all unfolding just as he'd imagined over the years.

He could tell his perfect princess had some leftover school angst, which was why he'd decided to meet with her estranged bestie, Emma, the next day for lunch. He wanted to know from someone who'd known Maggie well what had happened to her after he left for DePaul University to get a master's in business and marketing.

Of course, that was the story his family shared with everyone. Dean did get his degree, but the real reason for being in Chicago was to learn the business from The Outfit, the largest criminal crime organization in America and in the top three in the world.

Learning how to work the politicians became Dean's primary focus. The rest was simple mechanics. The more intimidating and the meaner he was, the more he could bully those whose job it was to fall in line. But, like Jimmy Falcone, he had no intention of being part of The Outfit. Historically, the DeLuca Family had separated themselves when they moved to Philly from Chicago in the early eighties, when DeFronzo was running things.

Dean's education was about avoiding the pitfalls of illegal crime but still getting what he wanted. It was dancing on the razor's edge. Jimmy said when you run legit businesses, you also need to appease the Italian Family connections. Both his parents and Maggie's had family members in The Outfit, so they needed to tread their legitimate path with care.

Maggie's behavior was crucial to staying low-key, and he couldn't have her gorgeous body all over the internet. When he'd spoken to Jimmy about it, he said he raised her, but Dean was the one to train her. And he had his work cut out for him. Keeping her safe would sometimes mean being an asshole, and she would have to suck it up and accept it. That would be the most challenging part, getting her to see that she had no choice and to relinquish her will to him when necessary.

Dean thought about the weekend. Maggie would be immersed in his world, in their life—the one they were creating together. But a challenge was required to interrupt their newly found bliss, to test whether she would listen when it was most important. Decided on a course of action, Dean took a shower and headed to bed, exhausted and satiated. He dreamed of a weekend of coital bliss.

The next day, he was deep in thought following his meeting with Emma. Being enlightened about all that went on back in the girls' young teen days between the two families made sense to Emma and explained her parents' odd behavior.

Emma had known that her father had done something terrible to Jimmy. Neither she nor Maggie was told what that was exactly. They had eventually drifted apart in grade eleven, after Dean had left, but the two still remained in contact on social media.

Although they ran in different circles, Emma talked about a guy who'd been following Maggie around since her thirteenth birthday party that he'd attended. Apparently, after Dean had left for college, the guy, Damon, and Maggie were often together. Eventually, he dated other girls in grade twelve but not before embarrassing Maggie publicly and continuing to stalk her.

Dean called his head of security, Mario Laduchi. *"I need you to run a background check on Damon DeMarco."*

> *Mario:* No problem, boss, you want recent
> history or everything on the Family?
> *Dean:* I want to know everything about this
> prick. I think the piece of shit is stalking
> Maggie and, if so, put an end to it.

Mario: Got it, boss. I will run the basics and do
　　　the Family. Give me a day or two to gather
　　　all the intel and get back to you.

Dean: That's fine. Also, Mario, I want a tracker
　　　placed on Maggie's phone and on her car.
　　　Is the security install finished at the house?

Mario: Yes, boss, it's all done. Are you worried
　　　about something?

Dean: Not worried so much as don't trust. The
　　　Marinos haven't made a move in a long
　　　time, and I'm concerned. And this Damon
　　　character gives me cause for concern, too.
　　　Get Andre to check through her
　　　Instagram and see if he's been stalking her
　　　on there. We'll go from there. I got to go,
　　　Mario, I have a meeting with Felicia
　　　Marino.

Mario: Okay, boss, you need anything else?

Dean: Yeah, I'm picking up Mags' engagement
　　　ring later today. I need a tracker small
　　　enough to hide inside the setting. Have
　　　Andre take it to Luigi at Desuuma's on the
　　　row and put one in mine as well. You never
　　　know when it may come in handy.

Mario: Got it. Later, boss.

Shutting off the phone, Dean entered the chic offices of
Felicia Marino. Never having met the woman before, but as he
was marrying into the Family, Jimmy thought it prudent for
introductions to be made. And Dean was not posing a threat
in any way to what was once a Falcone empire.

Dean was escorted into a private office in the back that
had a view of the river. The décor was very Italian, with gold
ornaments that were gaudy and traditional. But it suited the

woman behind the desk, who was as outrageous as her décor. Felicia Marino stood up and shook his hand.

"Finally, we meet. Welcome, Dean DeLuca."

"Miss Marino."

"Please have a seat. Can I get you a beverage, coffee, tea?" And then she smiled instead of saying *me* at the end of the rhyme. How very gauche of her.

"I'm fine, thank you. I have come to say hello and introduce myself, as I am marrying into the Falcone Family shortly." Dean sat back and took note of Felicia's eyes darkening at the name Falcone, but other than that tell, her expression remained impassive.

"Yes, I read in the tabloids that you and the Falcone princess are a pre-arranged marriage. How's that working for you? I heard she was more of an ice queen than a hot virgin princess." Felicia's hooks were out, and she was trying to bait Dean into a confrontation. No doubt an excuse to attack.

"Oh, I can assure you, she is warm and hot and, as of last night, no longer a virgin."

Felicia's eyes rounded for a moment before becoming neutral once again.

"I'm not here to discuss my bride. I'm here to say hello and affirm for you that despite my success here and in Chicago, I am not a threat to you or your organization. I will stay out of your way, and I hope you will stay out of mine."

Felicia's eyes observed him with a hunger he found discomfiting. He returned her look with not the slightest interest. She would be considered attractive to many men—an Italian Barbie doll. Not Dean's style in the least, and there were other ways to present a gorgeous body. His thoughts drifted to last night's fun and the first time seeing Maggie's ass without clothing. Her years of cheerleading and dancing had paid off. Her ass was perfection personified.

"Here is my card, Ms. Marino, should anything arise that

is relevant to both our companies. Thank you for your time." Standing, Dean shook Felicia's hand and left the opulent offices for the safety of his car. When he turned his phone back on, there was a text from Andre.

> *Andre:* Damon DeMarco wasn't hard to track.
> He follows her and has three other alias
> accounts. One of whom he has been
> talking to her, as a woman—Alice
> OniRam.
>
> *Dean:* What the hell kind of name is OniRam?
> Made up?
>
> *Andre:* I'm digging. I will let you know what I
> come up with.

A talk with Mag's father was needed to learn more about things that he'd been hesitant to share so far. As Dean was now in the need-to-know category, it was time for Jimmy to fess up.

"Hello, Mr. Falcone, Jimmy, it's Dean."

"I know. What's up, Dean?"

"We need to talk. I'm supposed to be picking up Mags at three today for our weekend. Do you have time for a quick meet at Gorgi's?"

"No problem, Dean. I'll see you in fifteen."

Whipping down to Jimmy's old neighborhood and parking out front of Gorgi's, Dean made his way inside. Sitting down by the window gave a view of the traffic outside. Dean preferred to be facing what was to come, rather than having his back to it, so he saw when Jimmy pulled up. The older man's physical prowess was impressive.

Jimmy was young to have a daughter of marriageable age. One could argue that he'd been a baby, raising a baby. Theresa had been on the scene just after Mag's grandmother

Maria had died. Mags had never been without a strong female presence. Maria had also raised Theresa from babyhood until thirteen, when they moved from the neighborhood. It was that story and what happened when college called that Dean wanted to hear today.

"Jimmy, thanks for the meet, sorry for the short notice."

"Thanks for the beer," Jimmy said after hugging Dean and taking a seat, also facing the window, but on an angle so he could also see the bar. Dean wanted to laugh at their similarities but wanting to keep this short and to the point, he opened the dialogue.

"Jimmy, what do you know about Maggie's life after I left? You know, at school, with her friends, guys, anything stand out?"

Jimmy's eyes narrowed and then changed to thoughtful as he considered Dean's questions. "She confides in Theresa way more than me. But nothing much stands out. She and Emma finally fell off the rails, and I was good with that, being Al is her father. Why, what did she say?" What to share with the father of the bride... less is more.

"Nothing really. But the happy-go-lucky princess attitude changed to the ice queen at some point. That doesn't happen by accident, and I'm digging to find out what needs fixing."

Jimmy glared at Dean with an intensity that made him wary. "Are you saying my daughter needs to be fixed, like a car that has engine trouble? That better not be what I hear right now, Dean."

"No, no, back it down, Papa Bear. Maggie is perfection, and I love her dearly. But she has a stalker from school, and I think there is more going on than either of us know."

"I'll fucking kill him. Who is it?"

Dean was concerned that he was losing control over the situation and didn't want that to happen. He wanted to make Maggie's world right. Jimmy had his chance.

"No disrespect, sir, but the time for you to fix any situation regarding Maggie is done. If I need help, I will ask for it. But with you having two small sons, I don't need to get you involved. I'm sure it's nothing I can't handle."

Jimmy chugged his beer and sat back, thoughtful, in his chair. "Okay, I will let you handle this, but I want to be kept in the loop, capish?"

Dean wanted to laugh at the old-school term. Still, Jimmy's father was straight from Sicily, and he was sure Jimmy heard those terms a lot as a kid, probably didn't even know how antiquated it sounded, especially coming from such a relatively young man.

"Can I ask you another question? You and Theresa, what happened to her after you left? You two are, well, you are incredible together, but once in a while, she seems sad. I think that is the best way to describe it. But something about her reminds me of Maggie when she tries to run away from confronting real topics, and I'm curious as to why."

An entire wave of emotions crossed Jimmy's face. "You are observant, Dean. I will be honest with you. Theresa and I, as you know, grew up together. In school, I was her protector, I imagine, a lot like you were for Maggie. When I left, all those assholes who had an issue with me took it out on her. Theresa became the proverbial whipping post for my bad deeds. Never would I have guessed that those shitheads from school would take out their issues on her."

"When you say shitheads, you mean classmates and others in the families?"

Jimmy nodded. "Them, and guys my age too. When Theresa arrived at my mother's wake, she was all I imagined she could be, except she had no self-esteem. I have been working with her on it ever since. T's capacity for self-loathing breaks my heart at times. Nothing that happened to T was her fault but entirely mine. If you're wondering what happened to

Maggie, then you need to look at whose care you left her in, Dean."

Jimmy had just slapped a big fat wake-up call on Dean's face. He was right, of course, and he had one more question to ask. "Can I ask you another question?"

Jimmy nodded his head in an affirmative. "How do you help Theresa regulate and gain her self-confidence?"

"That is easy. I love T and reward her frequently. I remove from her life what she can't deal with and do it for her. And lastly, I punish her when she falls into those self-deprecating modes, when they happen. At the beginning, it was almost daily, and now, very rarely. But as I enjoy spanking her perfect ass, I will playfully make up a reason, and she appreciates the attention."

Holy shit, the Falcones were into domestic discipline. Dean had always wondered how they managed so well when T was a strong woman and Jimmy, a very dominant man. Now he knew. As if sensing the direction of his thoughts, Jimmy spoke.

"My daughter is different from T in that she is way more outgoing and likes the spotlight. You will have to tread carefully, Dean. Mags is a Falcone, robust and independent. She will fight you on everything, and like her old man, trouble seems to find her. If you run the roost and keep her safe, then you'd better take control, now."

Dean had just received the green light to keep his future father-in-law's daughter in line. Oh, if only Falcone knew that Dean had already done what was just suggested. He'd heard nothing new but was relieved all the same. He'd received affirmation that he was on the right path with his intended. Dean's parents were a terrible example. He and his brothers, Peter and Andrew, had driven their poor mother crazy, and their father was happy to participate as little as possible. The boys were left to run rampant by their stressed-out mother, and Dean became the primary source of discipline, being more of a father than their real father had ever been.

"Jimmy, one more question. If you believe in spanking as a form of an attitude adjustment, why didn't you ever spank Maggie?"

Jimmy smiled as if the answer was obvious. "When T and I were young, we got into a lot of trouble. You could say I was the instigator, as I was eldest. I always took the blame for anything we did. And do you know why Dean?"

"No, sir, why?"

"Because I had claimed Theresa as mine from the time she was three and tried to feed me a birthday cake with her hand. She was a precious little girl, and mine. I didn't want any man touching her, including her father." The light dawned on Dean then. Jimmy had purposely saved Maggie for him, so he could direct their relationship.

"Thank you, sir. I am so grateful that you did. I never thought about it in those terms, but you are right. That is as it should be. I'm glad we had this talk. Also, Maggie and I will be at the new house all weekend. We'll be at the game on Sunday, and we wanted to invite you over for our first family meal, even though we don't live there yet. Can you guys come?"

"My boys would have that new white monstrosity of yours filthy in fifteen minutes flat, so how about I get a babysitter, and we come as a couple?"

"Even better, see you Sunday."

Jimmy nodded, throwing bills on the table out of a habit built over the past twenty years at Gorgi's. The men parted ways and got in their cars. Driving to retrieve Maggie's engagement ring gave Dean plenty of time to think over his strategy regarding her training and make adjustments.

Dean: Hello, princess, I may be a few minutes

late. I am just picking up a package downtown.

Maggie: Oh? In that case, maybe you should get a spanking for your tardiness?

Dean: laughy face emoji. You can try, Tesoro, but you may not like it when I inevitably win.

Maggie: Or… maybe I will? *The little minx was making him hard and uncomfortable.*

Dean: I will text when I'm a few away. Behave until then.

Maggie: No guarantees. Three winky face emojis. *God, she was such a brat, and he loved it. Training her to be obedient was like opening the best Christmas present ever.*

Dean: Paddle giphy

Hearing nothing back, Dean chuckled as he entered the jewelry store and rubbed his hands in anticipation of later.

Chapter 4

Maggie had a lot to process after Dean dropped her off at her parents' palatial palace. She'd grown up in the massive home that her grandfather, James Sr. had moved the family to when her father had been fifteen.

She felt that Jimmy and Theresa would have preferred to move, but they'd always left the decision to Maggie, as she had been born in the house, and they didn't want to uproot her. True to her selfish nature, she'd opted to have nothing changed, and they'd stayed in the home.

Maggie lay in bed that night feeling sore in all the right places and going over and over everything that had transpired between the two of them since he'd picked her up earlier. She knew her ice queen act was just that, an act. She had gotten so used to hiding behind the mask that it often appeared without her wanting it to.

She now realized that she had allowed her *front* to take over whenever she felt triggered and, as a result, hadn't been *real* with anyone for quite some time, including her family. Dean had peeled her layers apart in short order, leaving her breathless.

He saw her, every nuance, and it was so intense, it was almost intimidating. His power radiated from him like her father's did, and she found it heady. Her thoughts drifted to her father, Jimmy Falcone, and his childhood sweetheart, Theresa Romano.

Theresa had been a welcome addition to the family, replacing Maria and filling in a mother's gap for Maggie. There was just over a decade in age difference between them, as Jimmy had Maggie as a teenager.

Therefore, they were also friends. As Maggie grew up, she and Theresa had grown closer, and her relationship with her father, whom she adored, had drifted a bit. Then the twins were born. Maggie smiled as she thought about those two little brats. She loved them so much. They'd been the best distraction during the tough times in her later high school years.

Being in the pool with them and helping them learn to swim, their adorable birthdays, Maggie had loved it all, and during it, Jimmy had kept a firm hand at the helm. He let them enjoy their boyhood, but they could never be disrespectful to anyone, especially their mother.

Maggie's thoughts drifted back to the relationship dynamic between her father and T. She'd caught them one night, early on in their relationship. He'd had T over his knee and was giving her quite a spanking. She'd watched, until the end, unnoticed by the pair. It seemed Theresa had some confessing to do, and she did. Her father had been so kind and gentle afterward that Maggie had almost been jealous, and now, she'd experienced the very same thing with Dean.

He was solid and firm and very aware of his power. Maggie remembered when she'd been like that. Her thoughts drifted again to her thirteenth birthday party, as it had been a turning point. That day, Theresa had helped her discover her power, and she'd worn the mantle like a pro. She knew she was a lot like her dad and enjoyed challenges and being the center of attention.

When had it changed? When had she grown so uncomfortable with herself that she had to be an ice bitch?

Then her thoughts shuffled through her memories of school. She and Emma had drifted apart when a new girl to the school and Em connected. Maggie hadn't cultivated any close friendships beyond Emma, although she always had a group of followers around to fan her ego. Then she thought about Damon DeMarco. He was hot, very hot, and once Dean was gone, he hadn't left her alone.

The two had shamelessly flirted through the next year of school, to the point where Maggie had even considered disobeying her father in regard to whom she was to marry. Damon had kept pushing for the two of them to have sex, and even though she'd felt the desire, something had held her back.

She imagined trying to explain to the dominant Dean why she'd lost her virginity to someone else. But that wasn't even the truth. Maggie had allowed Damon to do everything but penetration. Eventually, she engaged in penetration with her vibrator, so she really hadn't been a virgin tonight with Dean, and he knew it.

She suspected they would eventually have that conversation. Just thinking about it made her want to run away. She laughed at how right Dean had been. She was very predictable. Feeling restless with all of her thoughts, she decided to take a swim, even though it was two am.

She threw on her bikini and went down to the pool. She dipped her toes and then plunged in all the way. After several laps, she gently paddled on her back, staring up at the stars. Thoughts of Dean and the sex from earlier came back to her, and she suddenly became aware of her surroundings in a profound way, really seeing the beauty of the night sky and fully immersed in the erotic sensations of the water on her skin.

She was turned on and wanted to play. Moving to the stairs, Maggie slid her hand into her bikini bottoms and leaned her head back. The water gently lapping across her added to the sensations. She fixed her thoughts on Dean and the gleam in his eye when he told her what he was going to do to her.

His hand had come down on her backside, which had created an unbearable heat in her core. These images and more floated through her endorphin-soaked brain. Maggie's breath hitched as she felt herself moving toward a climax. Dean's hands... his large manhood... *You will behave,* rang in her ears as she unleashed, feeling like a tornado taking off and whirling her until she landed.

Maggie released a deep, contented sigh. *Just keep it together, and life will be extraordinary.* "Yeah, sure, easier said than done," Maggie uttered aloud. Leaving the pool, she snuck up the back stairs and into her room. She had a quick shower and climbed into bed, falling asleep the moment her head hit the pillow.

Maggie groggily awoke at eight, to the sounds of her brothers pounding on her door. "Maggie, can you drive us to school, pleassse!" She was exhausted but couldn't help smiling at their whining. Her taking them meant morning car donuts, something their paleo diet mother would never buy. The pounding continued, so she got out of bed and flung the door open. "What do you want, you little heathens?"

Two sets of gorgeous, pleading eyes gazed up at her. Even at seven, Maggie could tell her brothers would one day grow up to be attractive. They would be tall, dark, and handsome. Both eyes went from her, down the hallway toward their parents' room, then back to her.

"Please, Maggie, we need some sugar or we're going to die." Maggie giggled at their dramatics. "Okay, but no acting crazy at school like last time, or Mom and Dad will find out. Promise?"

The twins nodded their heads eagerly. "Okay, go tell Mom I'm dropping you off today, and I will meet you in the garage. I have to get dressed."

The boys were already yelling as they took off back down the hallway. Maggie giggled again when she closed the door and went to her closet, choosing a tracksuit and runners, deciding on a run before coming back home. Theresa had been an Olympic grade runner and had gotten both Maggie and her dad into running. Both T and Jimmy had competed in marathons together. Although T no longer volunteered on a regular basis at LaSalle, she did occasionally for special meets, to enthusiastically cheer on her alma mater.

She dropped off the twins who were hyped up on sugar. Shaking her head as she pulled back out into traffic, Maggie hoped Theresa didn't hear about it. Then she headed to her favorite track, the one T had taken her to that first time to meet *David*. The park should have been a harmful trigger, but it wasn't. Instead, it reminded her of her younger, more innocent years.

She was hitting her first mile and remembering that day years earlier, when she'd felt a chill move up her spine. Someone was watching her. She could feel the eyes. Deciding to keep up the pretense that she was none the wiser of anyone else's presence, Maggie moved from the track to the center grass where she could stretch.

She bent at the waist, stretching her hamstrings and casually looked around. With every stretch she did, she looked but didn't see anyone. Then she remembered the bushes across the street. Lying on her back, with a bird's-eye view of the bushes across the street, she kept her eyes trained there.

Then she saw it. The glint of a lens, phone? Or binoculars, she couldn't be sure. Maggie gave whoever it was the finger as she got to her feet and headed to the safety of the parking lot and her car. She went home and was sitting down to breakfast when Theresa made an appearance.

"Thanks for taking the boys today. I have my article posted and done for the day. Now I can relax for a couple of hours before the little monsters return." The ladies laughed. Theresa sat down, joining Maggie in a late breakfast.

"So, how did it go last night with Dean?"

"Illuminating would best describe it. He reminds me a lot of my dad."

"Oh? How so?" Theresa asked as a gentle blush spread up her neck and across her cheeks.

Maggie wanted to laugh but didn't want to be so cruel as to call out T on her and her father's lifestyle choices. Then she thought, what the hell, they were both adults. "Theresa, you know I love you like you're my true mom. You are the best person ever, but cut the shit, we're both women, and I'm pretty clear on your and my dad's relationship."

Theresa turned a deep puce, and Maggie did laugh, then Theresa joined her. "He's, um, very dominant, your father. And, well, he is like you, Mags, a showstopper, intelligent, the life of the party, and my knight in shining armor. I wish I was more like the two of you."

Maggie nodded her head at all T shared. She was right, and hadn't she just come to the same conclusion late last night.? "I'm glad you didn't deny it. Dean is like Dad, very dominant. He has a treehouse. Did you know that?"

"Really? I had no idea. He had it built at the house?"

"Sort of. It's the childhood clubhouse where I went on my first time to the DeLuca house, the day you were kidnapped. His brothers and Dad helped him dismantle what they could and build it with some extras at our new home."

"Wow, I had no idea your dad did that. Kinda funny that you were the same age as I was when the Falcone Family moved. And now you're with a guy with a treehouse-like your dad had."

"Is it funny, coincidental? Or did Dad choose Dean because of the treehouse? Anyway, you know I always had a massive crush on Dean, and he is all that and a bag of chips, as I discovered last night. T, can I ask you something?"

Her blush had receded, but the roundness in her eyes remained. She often reminded Maggie of a deer in flight. No wonder she'd been such a good runner, then it hit. The two women weren't so different after all. "Remember when you helped me buy toys off the internet? Well, if I fully inserted the toy, does that mean I am no longer a virgin?"

"That's a good question. I think—"

"What are you two talking about?" Jimmy Falcone walked through the kitchen door, where he found his wife and daughter.

"Continue, Tesoro," he said to T, whose blush was back in full fury. Not having the same reservations as T, Maggie spoke up. "I was asking if I penetrated myself with a toy if I'm still a virgin. Care to comment, Dad?"

Jimmy Falcone blanched, but never one to back down from a challenge, he answered his adult daughter. "There are many schools of thought on that question, and I think many of the answers are culturally based, but the answer is no. It is generally prescribed that until consensual sex happens between two people, they are virgins. Toys are just toys. You're a virgin, or are you?"

It was Maggie who now turned a deep shade of red. Jimmy eyed both his women speculatively. Maggie pushed her plate away, no longer hungry. "No, Dean and I engaged in, uh, intercourse last night, uh, well, several times." Maggie closed her eyes at the sheer humiliation of sharing something so personal with her parents. When she cracked open an eye and looked at her father, he was smiling at her.

"Good for you, Mags. I hope it was great." Feeling tremendous relief, she sighed as she thought, *Oh yeah, Dad, Dean is fantastic. You picked the right guy.*

Jimmy's phone pinged, the tender moment broken. Glancing down, he saw it was Dean, wanting a beer. "Right on time, I have to go, ladies. I will be home in time to barbeque tonight, T. Until then, behave yourself," he said with a glint in his eyes.

Maggie rolled hers. "I won't be here, Dad, Dean is picking me up at three, and I'll be gone all weekend. Love you," she said to her father, kissing him on his cheek as they both rose from their chairs at the same time.

"I love you too, princess. Have fun, and you know where I am if you need me."

"Yes, Dad, I'm sure I'll be just fine."

Chapter 5

"**D**ean, to what do I owe the pleasure?

"Hey, Bobby. I just wanted to check in and see if everything is ready for tonight?"

"It is as you commanded."

Dean laughed. "I owe you, Bobby, anything, just ask."

"Hmm, well, I'll keep that in mind. I like the idea of you owing me."

Dean rolled his eyes. Theresa's best friend and now a business partner with Jimmy was always flirting with him.

"Yah, yah, you wish, just send me the bill."

It was Bobby's turn to laugh. "Good luck tonight."

"I don't need luck, but thanks." Dean hung up the phone and texted Maggie

Dean: On my way, princess. Be ready.

Maggie: Is that a command?

Dean: Do you want it to be, little girl?

Maggie: Ugh, you're so sexist! And I'm not a little girl!

Dean: You're right. You're a grown-up brat who
    needs a spanking.
Maggie: But I'm still sore from last night.
Dean: Then stop giving me a hard time. I'll see
    you in fifteen.

Dean hung up the phone and started the car. His phone beeped, and he rolled his eyes. He was going to have to turn the damn thing off to get any peace.

"DeLuca," he answered crisply.

"Boss, it's Mario. We got a hit on Maggie's phone. Someone else has already placed a tracker on it. We are running the tracers, but whoever did it is very sophisticated, and the signal is pinging all over the world. It may take some time."

"Does Andre know if it's Damon DeMarco?"

"No, at this point, it could be anyone. I have left you a couple of burners at the house. I suggest you turn off her old phone, leave it someplace where I can pick it up, and I'll bring it to Andre, or let me know, and I'll send one of the boys to pick it up. Andre wants to see if he can lead the mouse to the cheese, he said."

"I'm on my way to pick up Maggie. Meet me there, and I will give you the phone."

"Will do, boss. See you in a few."

"And, Mario, don't say anything to Mags. I'm going to tell her it's a generic search and I have mine done all the time."

"Got it."

They hung up, and Dean pulled into traffic. He was angry and wanted to hit something. Some piece of shit was stalking his bride-to-be, and when he found out who, he would end them. Then he ran over his plans in his head for the weekend and couldn't wait to get Maggie naked and in bed.

He texted Maggie when he was five minutes out like he'd

promised. He pulled up to the Falcone mansion and saw Mario had already arrived. He was about to knock on the front door when an Instagram alert popped up. Opening the app, he saw that Maggie had posted a picture of herself from sometime late the previous night. She was in the pool. But it wasn't a selfie. What the hell was going on? He walked over to Mario first.

"Did you get the alert?"

"Yeah, boss, Andre texted. That picture was uploaded by a bot account that could belong to anyone. He's working on it."

"Well, tell him to move it. That fucker, whoever he or she is, took that from Maggie's backyard, which tells me she is in danger."

Dean stalked away from the car, over to the front door and rang the bell. A harried Theresa showed up and beckoned him in. "Dean, so good to see you."

"Dean!" Two little boys came out of nowhere and barreled into him. Being the eldest of three boys, Dean knew how to play, and Jimmy Jr. and Leo loved him. Them showing up was good timing, allowing Dean to change his state of mind, so he didn't take his frustrations, unwittingly, out on Maggie.

"Hello, you little heathens, up to trouble today?"

"Dean, come and see what we're building."

"Boys, I don't think—"T began.

"I have time, Theresa. It's fine."

She smiled at him. "Great, thank you. You know how much they love seeing you. I'll let Maggie know you're here."

Dean nodded his head and then allowed Maggie's twin brothers to lead him out to the back. As soon as he was out back, his eyes traveled to the fifteen-foot hedge line and then the pool. He wondered how a photographer could have gotten photos. It was almost impregnable.

The boys dragged him over to what looked like the beginning of a treehouse. "Look, Dean," they said eagerly. "Dad is helping us make a treehouse, like he had."

Dean grinned, another generation of men and their treehouses. It warmed his heart, and he decided that if he and Mags had a boy someday, he, too, would carry on the tradition. "Wow, this is something. I hope I get an invite to the grand opening."

The boys giggled. "Of course, silly," they said in unison, sending all three of them into peals of laughter.

Maggie suddenly appeared at Dean's side. "What are you three naughty boys up to?" she asked teasingly.

"Guy stuff," the three of them said in unison, sparking another peal of laughter.

Maggie shook her head. "You guys are adorable, you know that? But Dean and I have an appointment, so we gotta go now."

"Aw, do you have to?"

Dean watched as Maggie leaned down and hugged her brothers, giving them each a kiss.

"How about I take you to school on Monday?" She winked conspiratorially at them, and they clapped their hands with glee.

Dean wondered what they did when she drove them to school. "Maybe I can come too," Dean said.

The boys' eyes rounded, and then Jimmy Jr., the more vocal of the two, said, "Okay, but you can't tell anyone what we do when sissy drives us."

"Oh?" Now Dean was really curious. "And what would that be?"

"We get donuts," they both said at the same time.

Dean laughed. "I see, so your sister is the sugar monster."

The boys thought that was hilarious. "Yeah, Mags, you're the sugar monster, not us."

"Maybe," she said with a laugh.

Dean enjoyed watching Maggie with her brothers. It reminded him of his brothers when they were younger. Dean needed to reach out to them. He'd been so caught up in business and Maggie and planning their future, he hadn't talked to either of them in a while.

They left the boys in the backyard. On their way out the front, Theresa emerged, looking less harried than before. "Are you two off?"

"Yes, but we'll see you on Sunday for dinner. Mags and I are cooking for you and Jimmy."

Theresa's eyes widened. "That will be lovely. Thank you, Dean. I take it Jimmy knows?"

"Yes, he does. Will we see you at the game?"

"Absolutely, the boys and I will be there."

"I'm playing too, so Mags will be there.

"Great." Theresa was all smiles. "Have a fun weekend."

Dean escorted Maggie to the car, opened her door, and then put her overnight in the trunk. Walking back around to her side, he opened the door and made sure her seat belt was on. "Mags, I need your phone."

"Why?"

"Please, I will explain on the way to the house. Can you just trust me?"

Maggie handed Dean her phone, and he walked over to Mario's car. "Here you go." He gave the phone to Mario.

"Boss, look at this. Andre took it down immediately, but another photo from this morning and another from last night. This guy sure is enjoying screwing with us, isn't he?"

Dean leaned down and looked at what Mario had on his screen—Maggie, giving someone the finger from the track in the old hood. The next one was of her on the stairs of her pool, her hand in her bikini bottoms. He sucked in his breath, going from 0-100 on the rage scale.

"Tell Andre to find that fucker today, or heads are gonna roll!"

"Yes, boss."

Dean stomped back to his car, his expression thunderous.

He got behind the wheel and peeled out onto the street, rage moving through him in waves like a living thing. He couldn't be mad at Maggie, as it wasn't her fault, and he hadn't told her not to be in the pool playing with herself. He knew she was probably thinking of their time earlier and getting off, but there would be no playing until her stalker was found. Besides, he owned that pussy, and she was not allowed to play with it. Only he was.

Dean schooled his features and slowed his breathing. Maggie watched him closely but stayed silent. When they were almost to their new dwelling, he finally asked what she had been up to since he dropped her off.

"Not much. I took the boys to school and then went to the track."

"What else?"

"There is nothing else."

"Yes, there is, Maggie, there is more, and you need to tell me the truth." Her eyes narrowed as if to challenge him. "Don't. I promise this is not a game. Now tell me."

"I honestly didn't go anywhere but the donut drive-thru place, to the boy's school, the track, and then home. I swear it."

"Did something happen at the track?"

Maggie hesitated. "Everything was fine until I got this creepy feeling that someone was watching me. I moved to the center of the field to stretch so I could casually look around. And across the street, in the bushes, I spotted a reflection from the sun reflecting off a screen or something. So I gave whoever it was the finger and left in a hurry."

"Why didn't you call and tell me?"

"Why would I? There was no danger, just some asshole checking me out. I'm used to it."

"What do you mean you're used to it?" Maggie squirmed in her chair. They pulled up to the new house, and Dean pulled into the secured garage and turned off the engine. "Answer me, Maggie. "Maggie looked like she was going to bolt.

"That's twenty, now answer me."

"Twenty what?"

"We're not playing that game. You know twenty what, now tell me what you mean, and I warn you, if you hesitate, you won't be sitting down for a week."

"It's just, you know, everywhere I go, guys usually stare. I'm used to that. Um, it never occurred to me that it could be a dangerous thing, and it didn't dawn on me to call you. But now that I know it's important to you, I will."

"Maggie, did I not specifically say that I wanted to know where you were?"

Maggie blushed a deep puce. "I totally forgot."

Dean smiled ferally at his wife-to-be. "That won't happen again. You can trust me on that. Did I not check in with you three times today?"

"Yes."

"So you had the opportunity to inform me and didn't?"

"Yes. But—"

"No buts. That is twenty more. Now, what did you do last night after I dropped you off at home?"

Maggie shrank in her seat. "I couldn't sleep. I went for a swim. How did you know?"

Dean pulled out his phone and looked at the new text from Andre. He passed the phone to Maggie and watched her face move through a series of emotions. Dean was playing hardball with her, but she needed to understand what was going on. He was going to keep all this crap to himself and deal with it. But his errant little butterfly required a lesson.

Maggie handed Dean his phone back with a trembling hand. She gulped and looked over at him. The ice around his heart melted a bit when he saw how upset she was. But the lesson needed to be drilled in first, then the rewards.

"I am dealing with this; don't worry about it, but we need to discuss a few things. I am going to lay this out for you again. One, you tell me where you are. Two, no more touching yourself." Dean leaned across and grabbed Maggie between her legs. "This is mine now, not yours. So you won't touch it without permission. And three, any issues, even if you only suspect someone may be watching you, tell me immediately. Do you understand what I have said?"

Maggie nodded, tears forming in her eyes.

"Good girl, now let's go inside. We'll get your strokes out of the way, put this behind us, and enjoy our weekend."

Dean went around, opened Maggie's door and helped her out. She was trembling, and he had a feeling there would be a fair amount of crying and sobbing with her session. Her guilt was coming off her in waves. Dean pulled her in tight. "Relax, Tesoro, everything is fine. The only thing you're guilty of is not keeping your word, and I knew that would take some time. You are not used to being accountable in this way, and it is new to you."

"I'm sorry. I didn't know."

He rubbed her back and talked in a soothing voice until her trembling stopped. "Are you ready?"

"Yes."

Dean pulled back and looked into her eyes with expectation.

"Yes, sir?"

He smiled. "Good girl, see you're on a roll already." Maggie cracked a smile and then followed Dean into the house and to their bedroom. "Listen, Maggie, this bedroom is our sanctuary. I don't want our bedroom associated with correction. So instead, you will get naked and come down to my office. I will be there waiting, you have five minutes. If you're late, you get ten for each minute, clear?"

Maggie nodded. Dean left then to prepare his office. This was not how he wanted to start this weekend, so the sooner it was done, the better. Maggie appeared at the door with one minute to spare. Dean breathed a sigh of relief. He didn't want to deal with any more behavior issues.

Since Maggie had said 'yes, sir,' he'd been as hard as a rock, and even though this was a punishment, he would enjoy spanking her gorgeous ass. "Thank you for being on time, Maggie. Please come here and lay yourself over my desk." He placed her hands on the other side so she could grip the edge. "Don't move, and you will only get the forty you earned. Move, and we start over, understand?"

"Yes, sir."

Good, he thought as he slid his belt out of the loops. He hadn't shared with her what she was going to get spanked with. But as he wanted to drive the lesson home, he planned on this being much harsher than what she'd received the previous evening, which had been an introduction and warning of cause and effect.

Dean brought the leather down with a loud thwack on Maggie's backside. There was a second delay, and then she let out a screech that made him thankful he'd gone soundproof for their home. He brought it down again, covered both cheeks, and watched the new stripe of red bloom on her lightly tanned skin.

She was so gorgeous, and he loved seeing his marks on her. He brought it down again just below the first two and made a new stripe. Maggie's ass was already jiggling as she tried to work out the unaccustomed sting.

"Stop!" Immediately, Maggie stopped shaking and stayed still. Dean brought it down four times, hard and fast. Maggie let out an ear-splitting shriek, and the tears began. Along with that, her shuddering breaths were coming out fast and short. Dean delivered three more. "Maggie, we're not even half done. Do you need a break?"

But Maggie was sobbing and crying and in no condition to answer him. Dean shook his head and wondered if Jimmy had done him a favor by never spanking his daughter as she had no threshold for pain.

"Go stand in the corner, Maggie. You have ten minutes to calm down before we move on."

Maggie released the desk, walked to the corner as instructed, and placed her hands and head exactly as Dean had shown her. He observed her ass, which was bright red but would be gone in a few hours. There would be no bruising or lasting marks.

When ten minutes had passed, and she had calmed down considerably, Dean told her to come back, but instead of lying over the desk, she dropped to her knees at his feet. "Please, Dean, don't make me go through that again. It was horrible. I'll follow your instructions, I promise."

How he wanted to let her off the hook, but he knew it would never work. "I'm sorry, farfallina, it must be this way. But if you're good and remember your agreements, you won't have to go through this again. Although that would be sad."

She looked up at him, confused. "Why?"

"Because, my little brat, I love seeing my marks on your ass, raised livid red stripes that show you belong to me."

Maggie's eyes dilated and traveled down to Dean's package, tucked away snugly in his molded jeans. Seeing his hard-on straining inside his pants, her eyes traveled back to his face, and she licked her lips.

Oh, oh, he was in so much trouble.

"Are you open to negotiation, sir?"

What was the little minx up to? "What do you have in mind, principessa?"

"I would much prefer to do something else with my mouth than screech like a banshee. So how about I lick that beautiful cock of yours, and if I ever miss letting you know where I am again, you can double what you just did?"

Dean wanted to laugh out loud. He knew this was her thing. She did this with her father, wrapping him around her finger. But he wouldn't reward her for manipulating him. He would be that guy who kept her accountable and rewarded her because it was the right thing to do.

"I'm sorry, Maggie, for as much as I love the idea of your beautiful mouth wrapped around my cock, you need to know that the manipulation tactics you employ won't work on me. I am better than that. We are real and will have a real relationship, no bullshit."

Maggie slowly stood to her feet. Even though she was tall, she still had to tilt her face to see Dean's eyes. "You are right. I have been running from everything and manipulating my way through life. It's so habitual, I don't even know I'm doing it."

Dean nodded in understanding. Even though he'd been aware of her in school and had watched, they hadn't gotten acquainted until she was thirteen and was already employing her manipulations. Maybe it had worked on Maria, her grandmother who raised her until that point.

"It's time to finish this, Maggie, I want to ravish your body."

She gulped and nodded and lay back over the desk, taking her position. Dean stood behind her and finished her punishment. This time, there was no screeching, sobbing, or begging, which he knew had mostly been theatrics. Maggie took her correction like a champion, and Dean was proud of her for that.

Chapter 6

The heat that seared Maggie's ass finally stopped. She'd promised herself that on the second half, she would accept, and by doing so, the spanking had hurt way less. The path of less resistance had been the right choice because something else happened with the last ten.

Dean focused his stokes on the lower half of her cheeks, and it created a heat that had her almost mewling with desire. She wanted him badly. Her hot ass just added to the myriad sensations roiling through her body.

She let go of the desk and pulled her elbows in, then she parted her legs so he could see what his attentions did to her. It was a bold move, but Maggie was feeling emboldened. Dean had shared that seeing his marks on her ass had turned him on. Now she was showing him that having his marks on her ass turned her on a lot!

Dean moved in behind her and ran a finger down her sodden slit. Maggie tilted her hips back toward him, trying to gain more friction. He used one hand to hold her hips still and, with his other, dipped a finger inside her and slowly pumped it in and out. Maggie could feel the heat emanating from her lower half, and his finger felt amazing, but she wanted more.

As if on cue, he unzipped his pants and took her in one thrust. Maggie let out a whoomph of breath as her belly pressed forward into the desk. Dean pulled her away until only her hands were left there. He held her hips tightly and took her fully and completely. No requests required, Maggie unleashed a torrent as she crested the wave of her first orgasm, shattering in Dean's grip. He kept pumping through the quivering and grasping of her walls, sending her bundle of nerves into overdrive. Maggie was no longer a thinking adult as she let go of everything and succumbed to his ministrations.

Her legs almost buckled with the intensity of the orgasms she was having. Thank goodness Dean was strong enough to keep her in place as he took her. Here, she loved his dominance, his complete control of her body, and knew she would crave it now for the rest of her life. He'd created a new awakening in her that could not be denied.

Dean's pace suddenly picked up as he expanded inside her, and with a growl, he unleashed his load, his hot jetsam sending her over the edge one more time. He pulled out of her and scooped her up, carrying her down the hall to their bedroom ensuite. He turned on the jets and then set Maggie down in the shower. He washed her entire body and then wrapped her up in a fluffy towel and carried her to bed.

"I'll be back. Stay there."

Dean hustled back to the shower to finish cleaning himself up and was back in two minutes. When he returned, Maggie was still sitting where he'd placed her. He stalked toward her in all his glorious nakedness.

Maggie watched his muscles bunch as he moved. His cock was already hard. She smiled and wondered if one could die from too much sex. She giggled out loud at the thought.

"What's so funny?" Dean growled.

"Just wondering if there was such a thing as dying of too much sex."

He smiled as he tugged the towel off her body and tossed it to the floor. "I haven't heard of that happening, but I'm willing to give it a try."

Maggie giggled again. He moved them to the center of the bed and pulled her into his arms. She marveled at how safe he felt.

"How are you feeling?" Dean squeezed her ass meaningfully.

"I'm fine, thank you. It feels swollen and hot, but it doesn't hurt."

"I guess I didn't do my job well then, did I?"

Maggie blushed. "I think you did your job and then some, Dean. I want to be what you want me to be, but I've been pretty free since graduation."

Dean drew Maggie's chin so he could peer into her eyes. "This is not about *like*, Maggie. You are exactly what I like, what I want. It's about safety. I need to know that you will respond to me without question when it matters."

She shifted to be eye level with him. "Of course, I would. Why wouldn't I?"

Dean rolled onto his back and sighed. Maggie could tell he was frustrated and couldn't for the life of her figure out why.

"Maggie, I know this is hard to get. But you have to obey me automatically, for your own safety. Do you remember the first time you came to my house?"

Maggie blushed. Did she ever. It was the first time she'd seen his clubhouse and the first time she'd felt his dominant energy. She'd acted like a brat to cover up how attracted to him she was, and she'd been so embarrassed by the intensity of her feelings.

"After you left, you saw Theresa, didn't you? She was

beaten up, but did you ever find out what actually happened that day?"

Maggie thought back. Her father had picked her up from Dean's place then taken her to Uncle Bobby's when they returned. Theresa had been on the couch, covered in bruises and bandages.

"Yes, I saw her, but other than my dad telling me there had been a hostile take-over and Al, Emma's father, had been part of it, that's all I was told. Emma and I were allowed to stay friends but in public only. Our sleepover days were over."

"Here is more of the story. Maybe this will get through to you. Theresa disobeyed your father and, in doing so, ended up being kidnapped and beaten so she could be used in negotiations to take your father's company from him."

Maggie felt the color drain from her face at Dean's words. "No. Really? I don't understand. What didn't she do?"

"That is their story to tell, Maggie, but I know that your father had to rescue her before the negotiations took place. Josh, Bobby's husband, found out more about the Marino Family, and it is this information that keeps them from coming after him, us."

"Holy, shit! I had no idea."

"I realize that, princess, and I share these ugly truths with you, so you understand what I mean by *obeying*. If something happened to you, Maggie, it would end me. That is how much I love you."

A tear slid down her cheek as she processed Dean's words, and she knew the time for holding back uncomfortable truths was at an end. She needed to be open and honest with Dean about everything because he deserved it, and she never wanted him to lose her if it would cause him so much grief. She imagined her father losing Theresa and knew that would be the worst thing to happen to Jimmy Falcone.

"Okay, I understand, and I am ready to answer truthfully anything you want to ask me."

Dean smiled at her. "That's my girl, but first we should have some refreshments. Are you hungry?"

Maggie had missed lunch and breakfast had been hours ago. "Starving, actually, I missed lunch."

Damn, why did she share that with him? Would he be angry with her? Dean's eyes darkened, but he said nothing, and she let out a breath of relief. "Throw on something comfortable. I have a surprise waiting for you, Tesoro."

She threw on another bamboo lounging set that she found in the closet, this one in white that showed off her tanned olive skin. She put her hair up in a messy bun and then found Dean in the kitchen. He pulled out a silk hankie. "Do you trust me, Mags?"

"Yes, Dean, completely."

He smiled at her response and placed the cloth around her eyes. Taking her firmly by the hand, he led her forward and then up a series of stairs, to a landing. Then it felt like he led her through a doorway, and she felt air on her skin a moment later. Were they on the roof?

Dean led her forward several steps, and then they stopped. He removed the blindfold, and Maggie gasped at what she saw —an incredible view of the old town and the inlet. But that wasn't all. They were encased in a garden that was mature enough to offer seclusion. In the center, was a table with a vase of roses. And to the left, a sideboard had been set up, with a small buffet, wine and crystal wine glasses, and water goblets. It was like being in a magical garden, and Maggie observed, awestricken.

"Wow, Dean, this is beyond spectacular. You sure know how to spoil a woman."

He smiled at her. "I'm glad you like it. Now sit, and I will serve you."

Maggie walked to the seat Dean indicated and sat down. He poured her water, then wine, and set them down in front of her. A moment later, he placed a plate filled with delicious-looking hors d'oeuvres on the table.

He took his seat and held up his wine glass. "To us."

Maggie smiled as she raised her glass in a toast. "To us," she mimicked. She and Dean drank and ate until they were stuffed. They moved to a little seating area that was meant for lounging. Maggie felt relaxed and unguarded as she sat in a big, overstuffed patio chair with her water and wine on a table beside her. She let her head fall back against the soft cushion and felt the sun on her skin. "Dean, I love this, and I'm never moving from this spot."

Dean sat across from her on a lounger, shirt off, his long, muscled, tanned legs on display in his shorts. He looked so good, Maggie felt heat ripple in her core. "Okay, you are fed, and now we talk, princess, and our topic is Damon DeMarco."

Maggie's' heat core went instantly numb. No, she couldn't talk about Damon. Oh, why did that have to be first? She played it cool. Maybe Dean didn't know too much about her high school flirting, or so she hoped.

"Sure," she said coolly, "what about him?"

"Don't play it cool with me, or you will be back in my office. I know you two had a thing going after I left. Now spill."

"You left me, Dean, a horny teenager. What was I supposed to do?"

"Excuse me, what are you saying? That because I graduated, you fucked some guy, and it's my fault?"

She wasn't and hadn't meant it to come out that way, but if it got her off the hook, then yeah, that's what she would go with. "Exactly. You left me to the wolves. It goes without saying that I would be pursued. But I never fucked anyone. I was a virgin until last night. Well, my father said I was, that vibrators don't count." She chanced a glance at Dean to find him with his mouth hanging open in shock.

"You asked your dad?"

"Yes, well, no. I asked T, but he happened to walk in and asked what we were talking about. I knew you would wonder why there was no blood and stuff, and in truth, I think my hymen broke with all the cheerleading. I penetrated myself with, um, a, well, a toy that T helped me purchase, and well, I wondered if I was no longer a virgin. My dad said it was pretty widely accepted that if you hadn't had sex with another person, then you were a virgin."

"I see," Dean answered, sitting back and looking perplexed. "You were a virgin. That is wonderful news that there was no other guy. The vibrator is surprising but shouldn't be, but now that I know your dirty little secret, I will expect a show."

Maggie blushed at the idea of playing in front of Dean.

"Let's go back to Damon DeMarco. What happened after I left?"

"He pursued me, of course. What did you expect, Dean? Finally, I gave in to his endless flirting, and we flirted with each other. He kept pushing for more, but I wouldn't. This went on for months, and then, finally, in our last year, he made his displeasure at my refusal very evident."

Dean was keeping his face blank. Maggie noticed, which meant he was probably furious. He'd been right when he'd said that she knew him better than she realized.

"How did he do that exactly?"

"He started dating Emma's new best friend and made a point of making out with her whenever I was around. When that didn't work, he would show up in places where I was. I never did figure out how he knew my location, as we weren't talking at that point."

Dean knew precisely how but kept his mouth shut.

"Then he started outing my secrets in public and shaming me. My core group dwindled down to a couple of girls. Needless to say, my last year of school was more nightmarish than one would hope for their last year of being a kid. He played football, too, and told the team he'd fucked me, so I became the school slut. And some of those guys had older brothers, your age, so they knew about us and assumed with you gone that I was fair game, I guess. Didn't your brothers tell you? I thought they would have as Andrew is one of Damon's best friends."

Chapter 7

Dean wanted to kill someone, anyone, at this point. His fucking brother knew all about Damon DeLuca and had never said a word. Heads were going to roll, including his twenty-year-old brother's. "Maggie," he said, trying to keep his voice controlled. "Do you know an Alice OniRam?"

"I do, and I talk to her often. She is in Toronto, Canada, I think, a nice woman who seems to know her fashion. See, Dean, I do have one follower who is into fashion." Maggie's attempts to lighten the mood did nothing for Dean. He'd been stuck on that name, and now it all came together.

Oni meant demon, or Damon, Ram was hardware or memory, and Alice meant noble. What was Damon trying to say? That he was a demon with a long memory and good intentions? Dean doubted it, and then he put the letters in Alice backward. Ecila—Alice in Wonderland, but more importantly, that name was strongly associated with the Kabalian in Ontario. The Canadian Mafia was quickly spreading around the world. The color drained from Dean's face as he thought about the ramifications of this information.

"Maggie, Alice OniRam is a made-up name and belongs to Damon. It is one of his many aliases."

Maggie blanched so quickly, he was afraid she might faint. Instead, she jumped to her feet and ran for the garbage bag Dean had brought up to the rooftop and threw up.

Dean, alarmed, also jumped to his feet and supported her until she dropped down on her ass. He handed her a napkin and a glass of water. "Sorry, my love, I should have been more sensitive in how I shared that information. Let me help you inside out of the sun. I think you need to lie down. I have an urgent phone call I need to make anyway."

Maggie got to her feet and moved to the lounger in the shade. "Dean, I want to stay here, please, in the fresh air. It smells so fragrant out here and it's a balm for my nerves."

A glint in Dean's eye caught her attention. "Swimming, I believe, is your favorite way to get rid of stress?"

"Yes, and I was always grateful to have grown up with a pool. Swimming, being afloat, I guess, is my favorite stress release. Well, second now." Maggie laughed meaningfully, gazing up at Dean with lust-filled eyes.

He scooped her up and held her tightly to his chest. For such a tall, voluptuous woman, she was very light and almost felt airy in his arms. "I have one last surprise to show you. I was going to wait for later, but I think it will cheer you up."

Dean carried her inside and down three flights of stairs, to the basement level, as yet unexplored. "Close your eyes and don't peek, brat."

Maggie closed her eyes, and when he told her to open them, she was staring through the glass at—there was no other way to say it—the Amazon, complete with a lap pool in the center and a hot tub. She gasped. She had never seen anything so beautiful. "Oh, my, god, I can't believe you did this. I can't even imagine what went into creating this space."

Dean chuckled. "Too much to talk about right now. But

you have Bobby to blame. I was all for a lap pool and hot tub, but he said he wanted it to be a unique space for you, so this was his doing. Do you see that wall of ferns along the back?" Maggie nodded. "That's the showers and change room. I have already placed several bathing suits in there for you, but as it is just us, feel free to swim naked." Then he gave her a meaningful look. "Maggie, you can swim naked here, inside, but no more at your dad's, no more playing. I don't know how the photographer is getting shots of you, but I don't want to see any more compromising pictures of you." Then he said *capish*, and Maggie grinned.

"You've been hanging out with my dad," she accused.

Dean laughed. "So I have. Now, I have a phone call to make. If you want music, it's voice-activated, so you don't have to mess around with any devices. Just say what you want to hear, and the music will come on."

She clapped her hands gleefully. "Yay. Thank you, Dean, you're the best man in the whole world."

"You remember that, princess, the next time I'm painting your ass red." His eyes glinted with danger, and Maggie felt heat bloom between her legs. "Be good," he said, turning away and leaving her to explore her new surroundings.

On his way back up the stairs, he had an epiphany. Could the surveillance be compromised at Jimmy's? Now he had two phone calls to make and hurried to his office, where he could close the door and rant without worrying about Maggie hearing him. She was scared enough, and he didn't want to make it any worse.

"Jimmy, it's Dean. Do you have a moment?"

"Sure, Dean, what's up? Thought you would be busy with your surprises."

"I was, but I figured something out and left Maggie to explore her new Amazonian lagoon. My guy picked up two pictures and took them down from the internet within seconds of the posting."

"Oh, of whom?"

"Maggie. One from your own backyard, Jimmy. I think your surveillance might be compromised. Someone is tapping into your surveillance to watch her and maybe Theresa. I haven't seen anything of her, but you might want your IT guy on it, stat."

"I see. And the other photo?"

"Maggie at the track, in the old hood, where you play football on Sundays. I know who it is, Jimmy, and I'm about to phone Andre to get him to bring it down. But this is attached to the crime families in Canada, the Kabalian. We need to look at who is part of that vast organization and who would specifically want to bring down you, me, or us."

It was dead quiet on the other end of the phone while Jimmy processed what Dean had shared. "Let's play dumb. They know you are on to a hacker because the photos have been taken down. Who is responsible for that?"

"Maggie's high school stalker, Damon DeMarco."

"DeMarco? Damn. I have some of the family working for me. Do you think this is just him fucking around?"

"I don't know, and I don't know if the two are connected. My gut tells me there is a much bigger plot unfolding, and we are just scratching the surface. Andre found out yesterday that someone put a tracker on Maggie's phone, and it wasn't yours. I figured this DeMarco guy was jealous and, for the most part, harmless. But after talking to Maggie today, I'm not so sure, and then his alias sent me for a loop, and it wasn't until about an hour ago that I was in the dark and then I figured out what his alias meant. I was about to call Andre but wanted to warn you first."

"Let's do a four-way call with Andre and Josh. He has

other databases he can check into, and he can work with Andre to get to the bottom of this mystery."

Jimmy waited while Dean set up the call with the other two men. When everyone was tapped in, Jimmy began with, "Gentlemen, we have a problem that needs fixing immediately."

Dean went on to explain what he'd learned and what had been happening with Maggie. He omitted his brother's friendship with Damon and the extent of Maggie's photo in the pool. Thankfully, Andre also kept silent on the pool photo.

Then Jimmy took over and went over a brief history of the Kabalian and the past decade of its growth and vast empire. After that, he went through what he knew of the DeMarco Family. When they were done, almost an hour had passed, and Dean was growing anxious to get back to Maggie.

"I have a question," Dean broke in as they were winding down. "Josh, can you set up a surveillance perimeter around the park tomorrow when we play football. Maggie and Theresa will both be there, and I want to know if we are being watched."

"Good idea, Dean. I was going to play, but this makes more sense. Maybe we can catch a break." Fifteen minutes later, Dean hung up the phone, feeling better that he had a team to work with and everyone was on the same page.

Dean made his way down to the pool level and found Maggie, naked, and in the hot tub. He quickly stripped and joined her.

"All done, lover boy?" She grinned lazily at him.

Dean dipped into the hot tub. "How long have you been in here?"

"Not long, about twenty minutes."

He sat beside Maggie and then moved her to his lap. With her feet resting on the bench on either side of him, her knees were almost as high as her chin. He guided her onto his cock, and she ground down, dropping her head back and uttering a long moan that tightened Dean's balls. Grabbing her hips, he pushed her down and began to pump his hips. Maggie responded, riding him in return. The water prevented them from a fast pace, but the weightlessness made the luxurious pace of their lovemaking perfect.

Dean dipped his head down and played with her nipples, circling the perfect tight tips with his tongue. "Being as you had a spanking today, little girl, you need to ask permission," he said, breaking from his feasting on her breasts.

Maggie's head came back up, holding his eyes with her own.

Dean got to watch everything she was feeling play out on her gorgeous face. Her eyes narrowed as she gasped, and he knew she was getting close. Time to level up her training.

"Sir, please, may I release now?"

"No, you may not until I tell you."

Maggie's eyes went from on edge to wide and surprised, almost causing Dean to laugh.

"Really?"

"Really. You are in training, Tesoro, and I reserve the right to deny you. You respond to my commands, not your reactions."

Maggie's grinding eased off, most likely in an attempt to stave off her fast-approaching orgasm. Dean stood, and her legs automatically wound around his hips. He walked over to the pool and jumped in, his cock still buried to the hilt inside her. She screeched when they were mid-air.

Once back in the water and weightless, Dean stood, waist-deep in the water. He kept grinding into Maggie, whose arms were now wrapped around his neck and hanging on for dear life. He gripped her ass and slammed his cock inside her, eliciting the most beautiful sounds from her dirty mouth.

"Please, sir, may I now?" she panted.

"No."

She lifted her head again and glared at him.

"I don't like this game," she pouted.

Dean outright laughed. Maggie's pouty lip was so childish, he couldn't help it. "Maybe you'd like a trip over my knee instead."

"Only if you let me release, otherwise, no, thank you."

The little minx was dictating terms, and that wouldn't do. Dean walked over to the stairs and sat down. Regretfully lifting Maggie off of his engorged cock, he turned her around and pulled her back to his chest.

Then he began to play with her nipples. He alternated between torturing them and feeling her plump ass grind on his lap as she tried to escape the gentle thrumming. Maggie was amped up and, as the minutes passed, pressed desperately into his hands.

She was almost out of her mind with lust as she twisted and groaned and squealed, captive on Dean's lap. Her squeals and moans were turning into sobs as her need for release grew.

"Tell me what you want, Maggie."

"Oh please, Dean, I need to let go, to come. Please, sir, may I?"

Dean had decided he'd tortured himself and her long enough. So he flipped them around and had Maggie put her hands on the stairs. He raised her hips until they were just above the waterline and then entered her quivering warm channel in one thrust. "Now!" he barked.

Maggie came undone, keening with her release, her walls milking Dean's cock toward its release. But she wasn't done. As her orgasm continued to roll through her, he took her hard and fast. When he finally unleashed, he'd lost count of how many orgasms his little minx had enjoyed.

The two collapsed on the stairs, catching their breaths.

"Hungry, princess?"

Maggie lifted her head and gazed at Dean lovingly. "I am, but I don't think I could lift a finger to help you cook anything. I feel like rubber, and even the idea of raising a fork seems too demanding."

Dean laughed, imagining her lifting a fork with a rubber arm. "Well, you see, that is where having a dominant man in your life pays off. I knew you would feel this way and had the meal already prepared. I will bathe you, dress you and place you in a comfortable chair, then I will feed you and wipe your gorgeous mouth when I'm done. How does that sound?"

Tears formed in the corners of Maggie's eyes. "I think you're too good for me, Dean, and I don't deserve you." The tears that had been threatening slid down her cheeks.

"Hey, what's going on, Maggie? Tell me."

"I always ran away from things, but those last two years of school, I turned into this ice bitch. It was because I was scared, Dean. I didn't want people to see me, who I really am. I somehow lost myself, and last night, when I was alone, I thought about all my avoidance tactics and the way I act. I don't like myself right now. I don't like what I've become."

He pulled her into his arms and then picked her up, carrying her to the shower. Once they were under the hot water, he stood her on her feet but held her close. Dean knew this would happen. He was breaking down her barriers, just like Jimmy had with Theresa. He would also have to build her back up, and that was what she was struggling with. She had lost that dominant spirit that was an undeniable part of what made her so special. Dean liked her brattiness and her quick tongue. Maggie was a leader and should be a leader, not some broken little bird. He couldn't wait to get his hands on Damon DeMarco.

Chapter 8

Maggie and Theresa sat on the bleachers watching the game. Having wanted some quality time, Theresa had taken the boys to Bobby's house for some fun uncle time. That left Theresa and Maggie time to talk and catch up in the sunshine. They giggled like schoolgirls as they watched the game, making snide remarks that only the two of them could hear.

Maggie appreciated Dean's fine physique. He'd invited his brothers to join the game, and the old guys played against the young guys. Maggie's eyes followed her father as he ran to catch the football. She admired him so much. "What an incredible athlete my dad must have been to still look that good and play that well."

Theresa's eyes were soft and filled as she watched Jimmy. "He's the best, the best man, the best player, my best friend... I love him so much."

Maggie looked at Theresa while she watched Jimmy and saw the love she had for her father. "You inspire me, T. You really are the best role model any girl could ask for. I'm so glad you stepped in and became my mom."

Theresa turned her teary eyes toward her stepdaughter. "That is the nicest thing you have ever said to me, and you have said plenty. Thank you, Mags, you made being a mom my greatest joy."

There was some yelling on the field, drawing both women back to the game. Andrew, Dean's brother and a year younger than Maggie, had just tackled Dean.

Maggie was off the bleachers and on the field in seconds. She pushed Andrew out of her way and dropped down beside Dean. "What happened? Where does it hurt? What can I do? Should I call an ambulance?"

Dean pulled Maggie down and gave her a big sweaty kiss. "I was just about to stand up, but this is good medicine. Maybe I should stay here."

Maggie glared playfully at him. "Seriously, Dean, I was terrified that something had happened to you."

He pulled her down and gave her a tight hug and a deep kiss. "Amo Bellissima."

Maggie forgot about where she was and deepened the kiss, feeling Dean harden beneath her.

"Hey, hey, there are adults present. Behave yourselves."

The pair looked up to see her father and Dean's brother, Andrew, standing above them. Jimmy drew Maggie to her feet, and Andrew helped Dean up.

"Sorry, brother, it was a lucky shot, and I didn't mean to hit quite that hard."

"You weren't lucky, Andrew, you're a good player, excellent, in fact."

"He is that," Jimmy added. "We're going to have to divide up us old guys with you young guys next time. I think the boys and I will be nursing our sore muscles for a few days."

"You're not old, Daddy. You're perfect," Maggie said, leaning in and hugging her father.

Jimmy beamed at the attention. "That's right, you shits.

You heard her, I'm perfect!"

"We'll see, old man," Andrew called out as they moved back into formation.

Dean chuckled and gave Maggie a lingering kiss. "Better get off the field, Tesoro, the game is about to begin."

As she turned to leave, he smacked her ass. If he'd done that a few days earlier, Maggie would have gone all ice queen on him. But the newly, partly restored Maggie wiggled her ass at him, making him laugh, and at that moment, she felt power move through her. She looked up at Theresa and grinned. "That was fun."

Theresa smiled in return, asking, "Is Dean okay?"

"Yes, but I want to kill his brother."

The ever perceptive Theresa said, "There seems to be some tension between the two."

Maggie sighed, "There is, and it's my fault."

"How so?"

"T, remember my thirteenth birthday party? There was a boy there you all liked, Damon."

"Vaguely, he was super polite, right?"

"Yeah, that's him. Well, he and Andrew were good friends in school, and after Dean graduated, well, you might say I got way more attention than I wanted from Damon DeMarco. Apparently, Damon is stalking me, and that is why Josh isn't here. Or, more accurately, he is here but not playing. He is running surveillance on us while the guys play. Dean told me to act naturally, which is why I didn't tell you before."

"So, Dean is mad at Andrew because he was friends with Damon?"

"Yes. That, and the fact that Andrew never told Dean what happened with Damon and me. We did flirt all through the next year, grade eleven and then grade twelve. Damon basically tortured me by publicly embarrassing me regularly."

Theresa looked horrified. "Maggie, why didn't you tell me?

I'm so sorry, cara mia."

"I didn't tell you for two reasons… one, you would have told Dad, and I didn't want him killing anyone. And two… I wanted to handle it myself. But I didn't, T. I forgot how to handle anything and learned to shut it off and avoid."

Theresa nodded her head sagely. "Boy, I know what that feels like. When the Falcones moved, life was hell for me." Theresa wore a haunted look before turning back to Maggie. "And now, other than the fact this asshole from school is a stalker, are you okay? Is that what your relationship with Dean is doing? Helping to restore your self-esteem, like your father did for me?"

Maggie smiled at her stepmother. She was still so young, but her eyes were much older, wiser than her years. "Yes, that is exactly what he does, and of course, he's been spoiling me rotten as well."

Theresa clapped her hands gleefully. "I'm glad you found your other half."

Maggie was about to ask a question when she saw a glint of light coming from across the street, opposite the park. She texted Josh with her burner phone.

Maggie: *Did you see that? The glint? Someone is watching us.*

Josh: *I'm already on it. Act natural.*

Maggie: *Yes, sir!*

She turned off her burner phone and smiled at Theresa. "What do you mean, my other half?"

"Have you ever read Plato's *Symposium*? It basically describes why we crave another half. It's an interesting read and way more liberated than the church view on connections."

"I'll check it out. It sounds interesting."

"It's the result of a fictitious conversation between the world's great thinkers. I always find it interesting to see how people think, and this was twenty-four-hundred years ago."

"Wow, so cool. I'm definitely going to check it out. So, how do our Neanderthal men and their attitudes of being in control fit in with Plato?"

Theresa laughed and kept laughing until Maggie eventually joined her. "That's hilarious, Mags. Let's not talk about Italian men and philosophy. They don't mix."

The game finished, and Dean, Jimmy, and Andrew stayed on the field talking.

Peter, Dean's youngest brother and only sixteen, sat down on the bleachers and guzzled down water. "Man, those guys are brutal. Dean and Andrew really seemed to have it in for each other."

Maggie was about to answer when gunshots rang out. Not knowing who the target was, the men on the field raced for the bleachers while everyone else was already ducking down.

"What the fuck is going on?" Jimmy asked no one in particular.

"Dad, someone has been watching us, but Josh is on him."

"Stay down, everyone," Jimmy demanded as they waited in anticipation of what would come next.

The minutes ticked by until Josh appeared and crossed the road, joining the group at the bleachers. "Hey, sorry. That was a warning shot. The guy is gone, and my back up gave chase."

"What guy?" Jimmy and Dean demanded in unison.

Josh looked at the group, no doubt wondering how much to share. "Some random guy with a telephoto lens was watching the game. I have no idea who he is." Josh looked at Maggie meaningfully, and she knew that Josh was keeping it generic for those who were not in the loop.

Dean saw the look that passed between her and Josh and she knew she was in trouble. She could have texted Dean on the field and told him, but she hadn't. Was that an infraction in his mind, even though they had been together? Maggie wasn't sure.

Josh, Dean, and Jimmy moved a distance away as the rest of the crew gathered their belongings and made their after-game plans. The few stragglers, including Dean's brothers, were catching their breaths and guzzling down Gatorade.

Maggie was about to call out to Dean that they needed to go get ready, but her engagement ring caught in the sunlight, drawing her eye down to her hand. Dean had officially proposed the night before. He had been very romantic, getting down on one knee after feeding her as he promised he would. When he'd opened the box, Maggie's eyes had popped wide at the ring nestled inside.

The band was yellow gold, with a three-stone setting. The diamonds were quite extensive, and the diamond setting looked like a crown. She'd loved it on sight and was glad it hadn't been some gaudy piece of jewelry that the Italians in her family tended to favor. Bigger was not better, at least not for her.

Dean had said it was a crown for his princess. So romantic!

"So, Andrew, I haven't seen you since graduation. How are you?" Andrew was taller than Dean, although he lacked the muscular width held by the eldest DeLuca, from years of honing in the college stadiums.

Andrew eyed her speculatively. "I'm sorry about school, Mags. I should have been a better future brother-in-law. I should have been a better person all around."

Interesting. Maggie wondered what he meant by a better person and felt Andrew had a back story that she didn't know anything about.

"That's okay, Drew. Everything changed for both of us when Dean left for college." Maggie had used her old name for Andrew. She knew it was a term of endearment that only his inner circle called him and, by doing so, hoped it would show to him that all was forgiven.

Wishing to know more about him, she was about to ask if

he was dating anyone when Dean appeared at her side. "It's time to go get ready, Tesoro. All good here?" His question was directed at his brother, not her.

"Everything is perfect, Dean," Maggie answered, although neither man was looking at her. "And I would love to set up a dinner with your family." Turning to Drew, she said, "Next Sunday, can we expect you and a guest?"

Andrew looked at his older brother, his open expression not the least bit hostile. "That would be great, thanks, Maggie."

"Wonderful." She clapped her hands. "We'll barbeque on our deck. I guess you've seen it already as you helped out with the treehouse?"

Drew shook his head. "Dean wanted you to be the first. No one has seen it."

"Oh my goodness, Andrew, Dean made me the Garden of Eden up on the roof. Wait till you see it," she squealed enthusiastically.

The two men bestowed genuine smiles on her that were so identical, she almost did a double take.

"Looking forward to it, but there is no plus one, just me."

"Great, then we'll have you all to ourselves."

Dean said it was time to leave and get ready and told Andrew he'd be in touch later. The younger two DeLuca brothers left the field, and Maggie and Dean made their way to the parking lot.

"Is everything okay? Did Josh catch the guy yet?" she asked.

Dean opened the door for his princess and strapped her in. Maggie wasn't used to being so secure and enjoyed the added attention she was getting from Dean. He really made her feel like a princess.

Chapter 9

Dean shared on the way back home what had transpired during the game. Josh had caught someone videotaping the game, for what purpose he wasn't sure yet. Josh's men captured the filmmaker. He'd been hired to take footage of Maggie. He would then develop the old-fashioned way and place the photos and negatives in an envelope for pick up. He was supplied through text messages from a burner phone as to where and when. Josh assumed that the guy taking the images would be watched and now compromised. But just in case, Josh would be supplying the guy with a tracking device hidden in the tape of the envelope for today's photos.

"At this point, Mags, we don't know how sophisticated this operation is, or if it is an operation or still only one guy. Josh is still digging." Dean watched Maggie out of the corner of his eye, gauging her reaction to all he had shared. Deciding to change the direction of their conversation, he asked about her conversation with his brother.

"Isn't that something I should be asking you? You two

seemed to be like two bulls bashing horns on the field today, and what were the three of you talking about afterward?"

Dean narrowed his eyes at his fiancée. "That is between the men. I will tell you that I was a little angry with my brother and giving him a taste of what it's like to not be protected."

Maggie's eyes drew into a slight frown. "Is that why he apologized for school? Because you made him feel bad for not watching out for me?"

"He apologized?"

"He did, and I feel like there is more going on with him, Dean. He seemed haunted, and I bet he has a back story that neither of us knows about. If I can suggest, I wouldn't wait until Sunday to talk. Maybe meet him tomorrow if you can. My spine was tingling when he talked, and that is my go-to that something isn't right."

Dean thought about that. Maybe Mags was right. Andrew could be in danger or know more than was safe to share. Dean would have to tread carefully if his brother was involved in this. He also wondered about Jimmy's DeMarco employees and decided to have Andre run his own background checks on the employees unbeknownst to Jimmy or Maggie.

"I will do that, my love," Dean said as he placed his hand on hers and squeezed. They pulled up to their new home that they weren't supposed to be living in yet. Dean still had his crummy, tiny apartment for another week, and Maggie still had all of her things at Jimmy's house.

He turned off the car and turned to Maggie. "This was a getting to know you, catch up type of weekend, and I feel like that has been accomplished. What do you think about staying, moving in early?"

Maggie's face lit up. "You mean I don't have to go home tonight? I mean, to my family home?"

Dean smiled at the happiness he saw dancing in her eyes.

"That is exactly what I mean. However, I would like to stipulate that despite the security, I'm not sure about you staying here alone, and Theresa is also home alone during the days. How do you feel about me dropping you off in the mornings?"

"For how long?"

"Only as long as necessary. Trust me, I want you in your new home full-time like yesterday, naked in my bed when I come home. I want you rested and happy, fulfilled. I want you to feel like anything is possible and all of your dreams can come true."

Maggie's eyes glistened as she listened to Dean. Everything he said having a profound effect on her.

"Maggie, what do you want to do most of all?"

"To make a difference in my trade. If I could, I would travel to areas worldwide with impoverished communities and find gifted women who want a fair wage for sewing my creations. When I get to the point of making my own line, I don't want my work manufactured in China."

Dean admired the way Maggie was expressing herself, her passion.

"Despite many sweatshops being liberated, there are still places considered unsafe for workers or lacking in wage. I don't agree with all of the U.S.A's manufacturing going to one specific country, either. I think it's dangerous, and our government is stupid for allowing one place to have so much control."

"And you feel it is important to take it to many countries instead?"

Maggie looked thoughtful as she thought over his words. "Not countries, precisely, but *communities* in need of a fair trade wage. My dad's cousin, Louisa, has a high-end store downtown, and she imports from designers in Italy who want to expand their brands into America."

Dean was about to ask a question when Maggie interrupted. "Yes, before you ask, you can shop online, but Tina tailors the fit for every woman, so her clientele comes from a narrow draw and is completely governed by spoiled women."

Dean laughed at Maggie's description.

"I would like to have two brands, one for the hipsters with simple designs and based on body styles, not measurements, and a higher-end brand for us Italian princesses, like me."

"Well, of course, all Italian princesses need top-shelf clothing."

Maggie giggled. "Let me ask you this. You have purchased clothing for me. Where did you get it?"

"Most of it was from online, to be honest. But I did go to Louisa's shop, and as she knows your body so well, it seems the clothes I purchased from her fit perfectly. And you're right, more and more, it is hard to find that tailored look without starting from scratch each time. I think you are on to something, and I would love to invest."

Maggie's grin widened, and at that moment, Dean thought she had never looked more beautiful. He was a lucky man to have scored a beautiful young woman with passion.

"Thank you. I will consider your offer, Mr. DeLuca."

"I could ask for nothing more. Now, my sweet, we have things to do in preparation for our first dinner. Let's go inside." Dean got out and opened Maggie's door. When she stepped out, he pressed her back against the car door as it closed. Delving into her mouth, he swallowed the sensual moan that seemed to come up from the depths of her being.

He gripped her hair with his other hand, devouring her lips, as she sagged back, allowing him to pillage her mouth. Her soft mewls sent shockwaves down to his hard cock. Using his other hand, he pulled her shorts down and slid a finger into her wet entrance. "You are so wet for me, cara mia."

"Huh," was all Maggie could manage, as her mouth was once again captured by Dean's demanding lips.

He suddenly turned her around so quickly, she almost fell, but he held her tight and then pulled her ass toward him. He pulled down his sweatpants and impaled her in one swift motion that had her screeching out loud and almost orgasming instantly.

Dean felt her walls tighten and spasm, but she held it in check. The little minx was learning control, and this made him very happy. He gripped her hair tightly as he sank his cock deeper inside her.

"Dean!" she cried.

"That's right, Tesoro, take my cock and ask permission. Do you hear me?"

"Yes, sir," she mewled.

Dean picked up the pace and began peppering her backside with light spanks. Maggie gasped and moaned, arching her ass for him, and he didn't disappoint. He wanted to take her in as many ways as he could imagine and moved his hand from her hot pink cheeks to her little puckered rosebud.

"Oh! Ohhh." Maggie went from surprise to lust in a nanosecond. Dean took her excess juices and slid his thumb into her ass. She was panting now, like she was running a race. And pressing back into Dean, she met his thrusts with her own.

"Dean, I need to let go. Please, may I?"

"Now, Maggie!"

A torrent released from her, soaking Dean's cock in her essence. He pulled out and replaced his cock with one finger inside her sodden entrance and one playing with her hardened nub. He pressed the head of his cock against her back entrance and waited for her to resist or complain.

Instead, the little moans and mewls affirmed that she was as into this as he was. He inched in while Maggie held still. Dean moved past the tight ring of flesh and fully inserted himself inside, remaining still and allowing her time to adjust while he played with her sensitive nub. He released her hair and, reaching around, played with her breasts.

Now Maggie had three entirely different sensations to deal with, and it was driving her mad. He allowed her to dictate the pace, so she began to press her ass against him, seeking a rhythm. Dean acquiesced and began gentle pumps as he continued to thrum and gently twist her nipple while playing with her clit. Within seconds, Maggie was ready, and Dean granted permission again. She gushed all over his hand, the tight muscles squeezing him tightly. Dean picked up the pace, seeking his own release. He grabbed Maggie's hips and began to pump harder and faster while she was swept up in multiple orgasms.

He released with a yell, pumping his seed deep into Maggie's backside. She shivered when he pulled out of her and slumped against the car. He scooped her up and carried her up to their bathroom, where he sat her on the counter while he ran a bubble bath, and then he stripped her and placed her down in the bubbles.

"You relax for a bit, beautiful. I'm just popping into the shower.

Maggie's eyes were already closed, but she nodded her head in acknowledgment. When Dean exited the shower ten minutes later, his lovely Maggie was asleep, her head cocked to one side. He was glad he'd sprung for the contoured tub. It supported her head and arms entirely, so he wasn't afraid of her slipping down and drowning.

He left her to get dressed, then he puttered around in the kitchen, pulling out the necessary ingredients from the fridge. A few minutes later, he went back to the bathroom. "Wake up, sleepyhead, your parents will be here in an hour, and we have prep work to do."

Maggie's eyes fluttered open and gazed up into Dean's

face. "That was crazy good. I feel like I've had a massage. Do you think we could order pizza?"

Dean laughed. "No way, but I will make you a coffee while you get dressed, and then you are required in the kitchen, little brat."

"And if I don't? Will the big bad mafia man spank my naughty behind?"

Oh, what a minx. Did she really need another lesson in the difference between a good spanking and a bad one? Willing to play along, he leaned down and grabbed her quickly, pulling her over the edge of the tub. He reached behind him, grabbed her stiff wooden hairbrush, and landed ten good smacks on her butt before she had time to protest.

"Ouch, that really hurt. What did you do that for?"

"I think you forgot the difference between spanking for pleasure and spanking because you've been naughty. I thought I'd remind you. Now, get dressed, and I'll bring you that coffee." Helping Maggie to stand up, Dean handed her a towel and left the bathroom.

When he returned, she was dressed in a flowing white jumper that highlighted her gorgeous skin color. The top hugged her curves, and the bottoms were like harem pants. Dean hadn't seen a design quite like it before. She almost looked like a belly dancer, except that it was all one piece and no belly was showing.

"I love that outfit, Bella. Where did you get it?"

"Oh, this old thing," Maggie said, spinning around to give him a three-hundred-sixty-degree view. "This is my creation. You like?"

"I do, very much. It's subtly different from anything else I've seen and not ostentatious like other similar designs. In this outfit, you could go casual or dress up. Wonderful for someone on a spending budget."

Maggie grinned. "Precisely correct. It is designed for

someone who can dress it down or up. I'm glad you can see that." Dean handed her a coffee. She took it from his hands gratefully and took an immediate sip. She sighed, "This is perfect, thank you, Dean."

He watched her drink the coffee, mesmerized by her lips on the rim of the cup. They were so sensual that it was hard not to look at them when she talked, ate, or his favorite, when they were wrapped around his cock.

Dean blinked several times and then moved his eyes to a safer place. Gazing around the room, he looked at the clothes strewn about and her wet towel on the floor. "I suggest, if you're giving tours, princess, you may want to tidy this mess up first."

"What, no maid service?" she responded flippantly.

"No, I thought I would like to see you on your hands and knees washing the floors by hand, and there are an awful lot of floors." Dean was kidding, of course, but the look on her face was priceless. "Be in the kitchen in ten minutes, Maggie, or that spanking in the bathroom will be a warm-up to the real deal."

"I will, I promise."

Dean nodded and left the room, shaking his head, wondering if she was going to backslide already. But when the doorbell rang an hour later, they were ready. Their home and the two of them all looked great, and all the prep was done, with dinner in the oven.

Chapter 10

Maggie put on her running shoes and headed out through the garage. After last night's dinner success, she felt she needed to run. Avoiding her favorite track, Maggie headed off into her neighborhood and the trails a few blocks away.

Dean hadn't answered his phone, so she texted him that she was going for a local run. Needing to unplug, Maggie threw in her air buds and put on her favorite workout playlist. She loved running almost as much as she loved swimming.

Once on the trails, Maggie felt free, alive in a way she never did in the pool. There, she could zone, but here, it was like her senses and her mind were two different beings. In one way, her pounding feet on the soft turf were very vivid. Her leg muscles bunching and expanding became a detraction that was almost mechanical. While her breath, her lungs, were part of a more significant experience. Her head filled with music that inspired her. Maggie increased her pace through the quiet wooded trail. She wanted to soar with her happiness.

After running for several songs, Maggie got lost in memories of their dinner the night before. Theresa had marveled at the house, and Jimmy had been impressed with Bobby's attention to detail. Then Dean had dropped the bomb, asking Theresa to share about how she'd been feeling up to the time she'd been kidnapped. He'd done it on purpose, wanting his lesson on obedience to sink in. She felt her father had been in on it because he proceeded to lecture both women afterward until Dean changed the conversation's direction to safer topics.

Maggie's thoughts were interrupted by an awareness that someone was near. She turned her head without slowing down but saw no one. She glanced to the denser woods to her left and then right and, again, saw no one.

She chose a loop trail and started her run back when the sensation blossomed into a person standing in the middle of the path. Maggie gasped as she came to an immediate halt. The person in her way was none other than Damon DeMarco. Maggie was breathing hard and trying to catch her breath after being startled.

"Damon, where did you come from? You scared the crap out of me."

Damon grinned down at Maggie. "I'm out for a run, like yourself."

Maggie's heart rate spiked. She knew Damon was lying, and she mentally bashed herself for leaving her phone behind at the mansion. Deciding friendly and stupid would be the way to play this out, she started to walk. "Want to join me the rest of the way?"

Damon regarded her in a way that made Maggie think of the big bad wolf. "Thank you, Mags. I would love to."

Maggie kept her pace moderate as Damon joined her. They jogged slowly at first as they made small talk. "I haven't seen you since graduation. Have you been away?"

"I have been, Europe mostly, but here and there as well."

"And you're back to stay?"

He regarded her with a look that sent chills down her

spine, but Maggie kept her friendly smile plastered on her face.

"An acquisition brought me back and will keep me here until I have it in my possession. Then I will fly the coop once again, maybe Italy, as I love the Amalfi coast. Have you been?"

"No, not since I was a kid and my grandparents took me. We visit my grandfather in Florida in the winter. But honestly, with school and design college and now getting married, I have been too busy for travel. Hopefully, before Dean and I have kids, we'll get some traveling done. Theresa says that no matter how rich you are, traveling with babies sucks." She laughed at her own jibe, hoping to keep things light.

Damon said nothing, no remarks, and no change in his facial expressions. That told Maggie that he was schooling his features and the man was in a dangerous place. She was about to ask him a question when he grabbed her arm, bringing their fast-paced walk to a standstill.

"Why him, Maggie, why did you pick Dean DeLuca?"

Maybe this was her chance to set the record straight. Perhaps if she apologized for flirting with him in school, he would go away. Mind you, he'd done some crap things to her but now was not the time to bring up those humiliating times in school.

"For starters, it is a blending of two families, two empires, that both sets of parents wanted, and secondly, I am in love with Dean. I have been since the seventh grade. I know you and I teased each other for a while and, well, other things, but it was never meant to go anywhere, Damon. I hope you understand that, and we can put that behind us and be friends."

Damon's grip on her arm increased, causing Maggie to yelp in pain. "I don't see it that way at all, Maggie. I see you as mine and always did. You are way better than Dean and deserve a lot more than DeLuca can ever give you. And I think it's time you made good on all your innuendos, princess. No more being a cock tease."

He was dragging her into the woods. She fought back, but the man's grip was like iron, and despite multiple kicks to his shins, he didn't relent. "Let me go, so help me, I'll scream, Damon."

"It looks like the fiery princess needs a lesson in behaving."

He dragged Maggie over to a fallen tree and yanked her forcefully over his lap. He was about to rip off her shorts and beat her until she was black and blue when he heard rustling. He pulled her shorts back up, pushed her off his lap, and gripped her hair tightly, bringing her to her feet.

"Maggie? Is that you?"

Damon released her hair but not her wrist, which was squeezed so hard, she yelped again at the pain.

"Josh? Are you out for a run? I just ran into an old-school friend, Damon DeMarco. Damon, this a friend of the family, Josh, and also a track and field enthusiast."

Maggie stopped talking but allowed Josh to see the fear in her eyes. It was not necessary, as it was pretty apparent that she was being held against her will. "Isn't Dean picking you up soon? You'd better hurry if you don't want to be late."

"Right, of course, thanks for reminding me of the time. Damon, it was nice seeing you again, but I really have to go." Maggie tried to pull her arm free.

Damon, who had said nothing through all of this, didn't relinquish her arm. "I don't think so, Bella. I think you're coming with me."

Josh's posture tensed, and Maggie was desperate to keep him from getting hurt. She made a move to wrench her arm free, and Damon snapped it. Maggie dropped to her knees, howling in pain, as Damon stepped forward and landed a kick in Josh's stomach.

Damon was like his namesake, demon possessed, and Josh, who was in excellent condition, was barely holding his own.

Maggie heard her name being called and screamed, "Over here! Help!"

Damon dropped Josh, then he reached down and yanked Maggie to her feet, throwing her over his shoulder and moving quickly for the deeper foliage.

Maggie continued to scream, and Damon landed a hand on her backside to shut her up. Whoever was following them was getting closer, and Damon became more agitated as Maggie continued to scream. He slammed his hand down on her backside again, and Maggie knew she would be bruised. When that didn't stop her, he set her down and hit her hard across the face, startling her and giving him a momentary reprieve from her screaming. He picked her up again, but it was too late. As Damon crested the forest onto the other path to make his way to the parking lot, he found Andrew DeLuca standing in his way.

"Get out of the way, DeLuca," Damon snarled at him.

"Put her down, Damon, you're out of control. My brothers are right on your heels, and there is no way you can get away carrying Maggie. Let her go."

The sounds of shuffling through the brush were getting dangerously close. Damon, doing the prudent thing, dropped his prize to the ground and took off running. As he passed Andrew, he said, "This isn't over, and you, my friend, have chosen the wrong team."

Andrew moved over to Maggie and helped her stand on her feet. "Are you okay, Mags?"

Maggie had recovered from the harsh smack to her face, but her arm throbbed painfully. "I think he broke my arm. Is… is Dean really in the bushes?"

"No, I totally lied, and he fell for it, thank goodness."

Just then, Josh came limping out onto the trail. "I've called for backup, but I see he is gone. Thank goodness you showed up, Andrew. How did you know?"

"I didn't. I was out for a run and heard screaming that sounded like Maggie. I made some noise in the bushes like I was chasing them and then waited on this trail where I thought whoever had her would exit, as the parking lot is just through there. Imagine my surprise when it turned out to be Damon."

Josh's phone rang. "Yeah, she's here. She's safe for now, but we have to go to the hospital. Her arm looks broken. Okay, will do."

Josh hung up. "Dean will meet us at the hospital. Andrew, can you drive?"

"Of course." Drew swung Maggie into his arms and started the walk to the lot.

Maggie protested, trying to explain it was her arm that was broken, not her feet. But stubborn like his brother, he told her to relax, that he was carrying whether she liked it or not.

It must be a family trait, she decided and relaxed in Drew's arms. Once she was in the car, he did up her seat belt almost precisely like his older brother. Maggie became thoughtful, tucked in the back seat with her throbbing arm.

The men talked in the front about Damon, and Maggie thought about the DeLuca clan. She thought back to all of her visits to their home over the years. Dean was always on guard, always watching out. She had thought he was paranoid and too controlling, but their father was never around, looking back on it.

He showed up for dinner most nights, but that was it. Dean, being the eldest, must have assumed a lot of responsibility when he was young. She thought about her father and T. It had been the same with them. Her father had been five or six when T was born, and he had taken her under his wing.

Maggie watched Drew's face in the rear-view mirror. His

resting expression was not as severe as Dean's but definitely more closed off. Whatever his story was, it involved a girl, she was sure of it.

When they pulled up to the emergency, Josh hobbled out into Bobby's waiting arms.

Drew was opening her door when Dean swooped in, concern etched on his face. "Please tell me nothing worse than what is obvious happened?" She saw in his eyes the question— had she been raped.

"Thankfully, Josh interrupted whatever Damon planned on doing in the woods. I think other than some bruising and scratches, my arm is broken." Dean scooped her out of Josh's car and carried her into emergency with Jimmy on his heels.

She was placed in a wheelchair, and as it headed down to X-ray, she glanced back to see her father and almost-husband in a fierce discussion about Damon, she assumed. Maggie sighed and dropped her head back, wishing for a redo of the day's events. She now knew that they were in a war, but as to how far behind enemy lines it went, she didn't know.

Maggie was determined to make sure she was never the victim again. Damon had made his move, and now she would do whatever it took to ensure he didn't get another opportunity. After a series of X-rays were taken and a shot of morphine given, Maggie's arm was put into a cast. She had broken both the ulna and the radius bones in her lower left arm, which after a few weeks in a cast, and physio, would heal without complications, as it was a clean break.

When they wheeled Maggie back out, Josh and Bobby were gone, with Jimmy, Drew and Dean waiting for her. They seemed tense but less so than when she had arrived. They wore the look of men who were laying plans. When they saw her, they stopped talking. Helping Maggie to stand, Dean asked how she was doing.

The nurse handed Dean a bottle of T'3s and scuttled

away. "They gave me a shot of morphine, so I'm great," Maggie said with a smile. "But I'm dead tired, thirsty, and hungry. Can we go home?"

Dean smiled down at her. "Of course, we can. Jimmy, can you drive Drew back as he is in your neighborhood?"

"I can," he said, holding his daughter gently in his arms. "I want the story, so you call me as soon as she is settled."

"I will," Dean promised.

They parted ways in the parking lot, with Dean thanking his brother for his intercession and help, and a promise to meet up the next day. He gently laced Maggie in the car and worked around her cast to secure her seat belt. The car ride home was quiet. He was clearly processing and thinking while Maggie was drifting. She was tired and sweaty and hungry and wanted to go to sleep, with the hope she'd wake up with the nightmarish day behind her.

Chapter 11

Dean had been meeting with Bobby and Jimmy, when the call came through from Josh that he was following Maggie's stalker. Based on her location device, Maggie was in the wooded trails by her family home. And according to Andre, who had at last been able to tap into Damon's cell phone, he was in the same woods.

The hair had risen on Dean's arms at the news. Maggie was in danger, and he needed to get to her. Jumping in his car, he cursed at the distance to the woods by her family home. Fifteen minutes later, he'd connected with Josh after a series of calls trying to get through, only to hear that she was safe, but they were on their way to the hospital. Dean swerved off at the next turn and made his way to the hospital as they should arrive at the same time.

For the first time in years, he prayed. The thought of Damon's hands on his princess infuriated Dean. His adrenals were working overtime, looking to fight, and he felt dangerous to those around him. In the years he'd been learning and witnessing the mafia's business, he'd only lost his cool once.

He'd gone on a bit of a rampage and ended up in the

drunk tank overnight. It wasn't his father he'd called, but Jimmy Falcone. Now, Dean gazed through his peripheral at Maggie slumped in her seat. She had dirt on her clothing and a few stray leaves stuck in her ponytail. Light scratches covered her arms, most likely from branches. She seemed okay other than the arm, but Dean wondered if she would have issues emotionally.

His bride-to-be was made of stern stuff, but she'd also been raised like a princess, and Dean wasn't sure how this would impact her. She must have been terrified. Josh said that when he came across them, Maggie had looked frightened. Dean banged the steering wheel, alerting Maggie to his emotional state.

Her large almond eyes focused on him. "Dean, I get it now. I understand what is happening. Until today," Maggie gulped before continuing, "I thought this was a jealous husband thing and you were overprotective. I see the bigger issue, and it's way beyond Damon and me. I see that we are in a war. I will make sure I am not a casualty again."

That wasn't what Dean had expected to hear. She was mentally in a better place than he could have hoped for. "Maggie, what about today made you see we are in a war, exactly?"

She stared back out the window. "He said he was in town to acquire a package, and then he'd be leaving the country, most likely for Italy. The Amalfi coast was mentioned."

The Kabalian was going to whisk Maggie out of the states. To what purpose? Or was this Damon taking Maggie a prisoner for his own sake. Or worse, did the Kabalian want Maggie, and Damon was working his own side deal?

"Did he say anything else, Mags?" Dean kept his voice steady and calm, the beast within at bay, although it was clawing to get out.

"Most of the talking was me, trying to keep him from

doing whatever he was planning. I kept up a steady stream of polite conversation. He asked me if I had ever been to the Amalfi coast. I said not since I was little and went with my grandparents, but he seemed to know that already. Dean, do you think my grandfather has anything to do with this?"

Dean thought about that. "I don't, only because I know how much you mean to him, and the Marino Family can't touch him because of the deal your father made with the Family. Unless Joe Jr. dies, then Jimmy's leverage is gone. I need to do some digging." Dean didn't want to, but he had to ask. "Maggie, did he touch you or molest you in any way?"

"Just before Josh showed up, Damon was about to beat my ass black and blue, or so he said as he pulled me over his lap on a log and was about to rip my shorts down. When Damon heard Josh, he yanked my shorts up and dropped me on the ground. He lifted me by my hair. My scalp is still tingling. When I tried to get away, he snapped my arm and dropped Josh like a sack of potatoes. Then he threw me over his shoulder. If your brother hadn't been on the other trail when Damon came out of the woods, I wouldn't be here."

The image in Dean's mind made him see red, but he had to stay calm and get Maggie home and safe. He'd had Mario station extra security, and his house would now be like Fort Knox and under constant camera surveillance.

Once they were home, Dean wrapped up Maggie's arm and took her into the shower, where he washed every inch of her body and her hair. He put her to bed and brought her water to drink and food. Then he watched her nod off to sleep.

Dean left her then and went to his office, where he called Jimmy. He brought him up to speed on what Maggie had shared. "Who are we connected to on the Almalfi coast, Jimmy?"

"No one that I know of. Maybe this little shit is using that line to distract us. I pulled in Damon's family members who work for my organization. They swear up and down they didn't even know Damon was in the country. They say he went rogue right after school, and no one has seen him."

"We need to find out where he flew in from. Is that something Josh can do?"

"It is, and he's on it already. What about your brother, Dean? Why was he there? He is hiding something. I just know it."

"Yeah, I called him. He is coming over tonight, and before he does, I have to work out. If I don't punch something, I'm going to explode."

"I understand that feeling. How is my princess?"

"She is better than I could have hoped for. There are two bruises on her in the shape of that piece of shit's hand. But she sees this for what it is, war. Maggie won't do anything stupid after today. The consequences of her actions are as vivid as that broken arm of hers. She's sleeping now."

"Good, unless something important comes up tonight, we'll chat tomorrow. T wants to come over and see her, and her brothers do too."

"No problem, we'll see you tomorrow." Dean hung up the phone and checked in on Maggie before going down to the gym. He was glad Bobby had talked him into the workout space. As he maneuvered around the bag he was punching, he pictured Damon DeMarco's face from school. The little shit-head had been an arrogant punk back then, fooling everyone into thinking he was a wonderful, polite kid, but Dean had seen the demon, even back then.

He'd warned Maggie to stay away from him, but Maggie said she and Damon flirted after Dean graduated. He was hoping his brother would shed some light on the dynamics of Damon and Maggie. Maybe Jimmy was right. Maybe Drew did know more than he'd shared so far.

Dean jumped in the pool when he was done beating the image of Damon's face on the bag. He swam sixty lengths before exiting and finally felt the crazy adrenalin from earlier vanish. He showered in the poolroom and threw on new clothing, another one of Bobby's suggestions, to keep extra sets of loungewear in the change room. Now he saw the intelligence of the idea. He didn't have to risk waking up Maggie, who needed the sleep to repair.

Dean was in the kitchen when he was alerted his brother had arrived. Letting him in, he grabbed some drinks and took him upstairs to the roof. It was a beautiful night, and Dean wanted to keep in mind that his brother was not his enemy even if he might be in bed with one.

Dean noted that Drew's eyes were constantly taking in his surroundings as they moved through the house. When they finally arrived on the roof, Drew whistled. "Wow, you really built your princess a castle, didn't you, bro?"

Dean smiled. "Yeah, I guess you could say that, and the castle now has extra guards to keep the princess safe."

Drew turned toward him. "How is Maggie doing?"

"She's resting. I have to thank you once again. Maggie shared that she would be gone, kidnapped, and probably out of the country if it weren't for you being there."

Drew nodded but remained silent. Dean knew his brother well, had watched Drew go from a fun kid, the craziest of the three of them, into someone different. Since he'd been back, his brother's darkness had bothered him, and tonight, he planned on finding out the truth of what had happened to Drew and his part in the DeMarco Family.

Both men stared into the night, into the treasure chest of lights that made up the Philadelphia skyline.

"Drew, you need to tell me what is going on. I know you're holding back, and Maggie knows it too. I promise that no matter how bad it is or how deep into enemy territory you are, I will help you."

Drew's facial expression didn't alter in any way with Dean's pronouncement, but his eyes no longer held a guarded look.

"What happened after I left school? When did you become best buddies with Damon?"

Drew smiled, a sad lift of one corner of his mouth. "It's a pathetic tale, brother, are you sure you want to hear it?

"I do."

"Okay, when you left, nothing much changed for me except that my anchor had been uprooted. I know I was fifteen when you left. I should have had my shit together. But you were always there, always had my back. You asked me to look out for Maggie, and at first, I did. Well, I tried."

Drew threw back the remnants of his beer, and Dean handed him another. "Anyway, the cheerleaders became the hot thing that year, and Maggie and Emma were the leaders. They seemed to take on their leadership role pretty seriously, and being a year older than myself, they had charm and smarts and were way out of my league. I had a crush on Emma through school, and Damon had one on Maggie. He told me he could get Emma to fall for me if I ran some errands for her father."

Dean's heart froze. Oh no, his brother had been helping out the Falcone enemy. Dean hoped that he would be able to save him from Jimmy.

"Damon took me to Emma's one day, and I met Al. I won't offer any excuses, but I was unaware of what had happened between the two families. I didn't find out until we moved the treehouse and you and Mr. Falcone were talking about it. I have been trying ever since to get out, but Damon and his crew won't let me. I'm a walking dead man, brother, because of today. Damon won't let me off the hook. He went after

Maggie because he wants her, yes, but I don't think he would have tried to take her so blatantly if not for me. He is teaching me a lesson. If I try to segregate, my family will pay."

"What have you been doing for the Marinos?" Dean was dreading the answer, but they might as well pull the Band-Aid off all the way.

"After school, when I didn't have football practice, I was an errand boy, but for Al, not the Marinos."

"I fail to see the difference, as Al is Felicia Marino's number two."

"I know he is, but he does other stuff too."

Now it was getting interesting. It looked like Al was playing his new boss, just like he had Jimmy. "Tell me everything you know. This could be our ticket to winning the war. You realize we have been in the dark trying to figure out if Damon is acting on his own or part of a much larger scene."

"I don't know how much I can tell you as I primarily work with Al, and then he made Damon his number two, and they have been doing things that I am not privy to. Al has had Damon flying around the world for him, though, and he spends a lot of time in Ontario, Canada and then in Italy, but he's also been to the middle east. Whatever he is up to, I'm sure the Marino Family knows nothing about it."

"That fucker sure likes to screw around those he is supposed to be loyal to. Damn Al Carbone."

"He's not a Carbone. Although he is related to them, Al is a Siderna. He spearheads a branch of the Ndrangheta clan here in Philadelphia and works with his namesake in Italy. I think that is why Damon is away so much. He is lubricating the relationships for Al, who is still playing the dumb number two for the Marino Family."

Dean couldn't believe what he was hearing. This was so much bigger than he had first thought. "Drew, how deep in this are you?"

"I'm not, brother, this is Damon wanting to fuck with you. I think that was his plan back in school. The deal was I do errands for Al to get close to Emma, but what actually happened was I was busy and out of the way, and he spent that time flirting and hanging out with Maggie. It took a while to find that out, and eventually, it was Emma who happened to ask one day if you and Maggie were still intended as she seemed totally into Damon."

Dean's hands curled into fists. Damon had to die. There was no other way around it. "What did he say to you when he ran earlier today?"

"That I'd picked the wrong side. Damon is gunning for me now because I helped Maggie. I'm sorry, brother, for my part, but with or without me, this would still be happening. The man wants Maggie, and he won't stop until he gets her."

"I understand, and I will deal with it with him. Now give me a rundown of your days at Penn University. I need you to give me a schedule of classes and your football games."

Drew laughed. "It's summer, Dean. All I have right now is football camp and the odd errand for Al or Damon."

"That needs to end, Drew, and I will make sure you stay safe. In the meantime, I could certainly use you. Do you want to work for your older bro?"

Drew offered Dean his first genuine smile in ages. "I thought you'd never ask."

"Good. Let's start off by you giving me your phone. I have a stack of burners with tracking chips, so if anything happens, we can still find you."

Drew and Dean left the roof and headed for Dean's office. Once Drew's phone was set up, they called Andre, and Dean put two full-time security men on his brother. When they parted two hours later, Dean felt good about the situation for the first time in days.

Chapter 12

Maggie woke up when Dean entered the bedroom to check on her. She stretched and felt the pain immediately, letting out a sharp hiss of breath. "Remind me not to stretch my arm. It hurts when I do."

Dean smiled at her. "I have brought you food and drugs. That should help." He helped her move into a seated position, and then he placed the food in front of her. Thankfully, she'd broken her left arm and was right-handed, so she could still perform many things on her own. "I just had a meeting with my brother. I understand what is happening now," he informed her.

Maggie signed for him to continue while she ate. "This all comes back to Al. He is screwing over his employers, the Marino Family."

"Seriously," she mumbled through a mouthful of grilled cheese. "Why is it Al always seems to be at the head of everything that goes wrong with my Family?"

"That is a good question," Dean said, wiping a crumb off her soft lips. "Do you think Emma knows anything?"

Maggie swallowed and sat back. "That is also a good question. I've been thinking about inviting her here for dinner or lunch. I know she is the daughter of, clearly, the worst man ever. But she was my bestie, and I really miss her."

"Yeah, well, you're not the only one. Apparently, Drew has been pining for her since kindergarten."

"Really?" Maggie giggled. "Aww, that is so cute."

"Not really, but he is still in love with her, poor guy."

"Why poor guy? Why aren't they dating?"

Maggie finished her soup and sandwich while Dean gave her a rundown of what Drew had shared with him, and while he shared, an idea formulated regarding her erstwhile friend and soon-to-be brother. "So let's test her. We'll invite Ems for dinner on Sunday with Drew, but we won't tell either of them. I'll get hold of her phone, and you can put a tap on it. We can check into her communications and see if she is in the loop. And if not, bring her into our fold, Dean. I would love to have Emma with us and your brother rather than left with her father."

Dean sighed. "For you, cara mia, I will have her here on Sunday. But she will have to go through a search before entering our premises, is that clear? And," Dean interrupted Maggie before she agreed, "If she is clear, then I will consider the rest of your request." Maggie was about to switch into her manipulation role when Dean held up his hand. "Unless you want me to tenderize that perfect ass of yours, I suggest you keep quiet and accept my deal."

Maggie was learning how to pick her battles, and this was not the time. "And if I'm a good girl and do what you say, will I get a reward?" Maggie licked her lips suggestively and watched as Dean's cock hardened against his pants. She almost felt giddy with power at her ability to get him hard so quickly.

Dean grabbed hold of her ankles and slowly slid her down the bed. He removed the precariously placed tray and then parted her legs. He moved between them and began to play with her seam, gently teasing her entrance.

Maggie shifted her ass to make herself more accessible to him. Then she pressed her knees as far apart as they would go. Dean continued to play with her entrance while Maggie wiggled impatiently.

Dean laughed out loud, and Maggie's head snapped up to glare down at him. "Seriously, DeLuca, fuck that pussy!"

Dean gazed up at her, his face unreadable. He wrapped his hands around her ankles and gave a sudden tug, eliciting a small scream at the suddenness. "Maybe now is a good time to address the fact that you didn't take your cell phone on your run with you, hmm?"

"B-but I, ah, oh, please, Dean, please don't. I won't say a word, I promise."

Dean didn't listen to her. Instead, he gently placed her over his lap and pushed up her nightgown. She felt him drawing the outline of the handprint with his finger. Poor Dean, he must be so upset, seeing another man's mark on her.

Not wanting her attacker's image to infiltrate their bedroom, Dean shut off his subsequent thought and instead began to lightly pepper her backside, giving her a gentle warm-up. After the first few, Maggie totally relaxed. She moaned lightly like a kitten, and after a few minutes of gently tapping her ass to a perfect rosy pink, Maggie felt Dean's hard-on pressing painfully into the front of her hip.

He moved his hand between her legs and delved in two fingers, pumping and hitting her G-spot. Her moans grew into cries as she fought the tightening and spasming of her inner walls, but she hung on. She wanted to show Dean how good she had gotten at controlling her reactions.

Maggie's cries were hitching. "Dean, please, may I?" He granted permission, and she became unhinged, riding the ecstasy wave as Dean continued wringing one orgasm after another from her body. When she thought she could take no more, he switched her position and entered her in one thrust. Maggie screeched with the assault and did her best to return his thrusts. She loved being taken by Dean.

The louder she was with expressing her pleasure, the more he seemed to grow inside her. She felt him swell, and his thrusts become more animated, then he released with a roar that sent Maggie over the edge one more time. When they caught their breaths, he placed her back in the bed and went for a washcloth. Her eyes were partially closed when he came back to the bed to wipe her and tuck her in. She smiled up at his handsome face and then promptly fell asleep.

Chapter 13

Jimmy Falcone sat in Gorgi's waiting for Dean. He wasn't surprised when Drew walked through the door with his older brother. He knew the younger DeLuca was involved somehow, and now he knew Dean had brought him so he could hear everything for himself.

An hour later, Jimmy was ready to hunt down and kill Al. "How the hell did he manage to cover up his true identity all these years? His dad is my dad's best friend and has been for the past forty years."

Dean and Drew remained silent, but both looked meaningfully at Jimmy. "You two think my pops is in on this? There is no way he would allow anyone to hurt Maggie."

Dean spoke up. "I don't think Damon trying to kidnap Maggie has anything to do with what else is happening here. There is a larger war being waged, Jimmy. The situation with Damon would have happened regardless, and the shithead is using the Kabalian to hide his actions behind."

"How else could Al be a Siderna, without your knowledge? Surely, your father would know?" Drew asked gently. "Or Al has been overlooked as a criminal mastermind."

Jimmy thought about Al, the son of his father's best friend. "I think Al is the ultimate opportunist, or I did when he worked against me for the Marino Family. What I could never understand was why. He made just as much money with me if that was what he wanted. With Felicia in the way, he can't be number one, and Joseph Marino wouldn't make him number one if something happened to Felicia. He would send someone from Sicily."

"Maybe it has nothing to do with money, Jimmy. Perhaps the point was to knock down the kingpins. With Al and Damon here, don't you think they are aiming to create a power hub? They are moving into parts of Europe and Africa. They will be on every continent, and when they are, then the smaller families would be wiped out, wouldn't they?"

Jimmy looked at Dean like he'd grown two heads. "Holy shit! You're right. I can't believe this has been going on under my nose, all of our noses. Security isn't going to keep any of us safe, boys. It's time to go on the offensive."

"Agreed," the DeLuca men said in unison.

"I need to meet with Felicia Marino, the Merlino Family, and the Lambinis today. We need a plan, something we can present to them that will give us a truce while we take down the threat."

"Jimmy, we have to include the Five Families. They have branches in Jersey, Pittsburgh, and New England."

"And The Outfit. We need to talk to them, too," Drew added. The three men sat back with a sigh.

"Okay, we will call a meeting with the Family heads some-where neutral. Maine?"

"No, they are connected. New Hampshire, all of New England, is part of the Five Families.

"Let's meet in Ohio," Drew suggested. "The families there have lost most of their power, it is straggling, and we won't be attacked. Everything else is too close to the Canadian border, where our enemies are building."

"Okay," Jimmy said, "that is a good plan. Let's get this done sooner rather than later. Dean, you'd better let your father know what's going on and talk to Chicago. I will talk to the Five Families and the Marinos. Listen, boys, we need to keep up the pretense that we aren't on to them. I'm going to talk to Josh and Gigliotti. I want documentation drawn up when we make our agreements for a temporary truce."

Jimmy was worried about his family while they worked out their plan and executed it. He had to think about the safest place to put them while he and Dean worked to clean up the massive shit pile created by Al and his crew.

"Drew, can you find a way to cut off from Damon without alerting him to our plan?"

"What are you thinking, Mr. Falcone?"

"Jimmy, please, and I think that I want to throw them a bone. I want it leaked to Damon and the Serenas that my family is going to Florida to meet up with my father. We need them protected, and I will have Josh put them in a witness protection location until our plan is in motion."

Dean didn't look happy but kept his mouth shut. "Do you really think that is necessary, Jimmy? My place is a fortress. No one is getting in there, and no offense, but your place has too many weaknesses. I know your father built it to show off wealth, but my place was built to house my queen. With the tech I have and the panic room, no one is getting to Maggie."

"Good point, Dean. We will move in with you until this is over."

Drew laughed at the pronouncement, Jimmy and Dean joining him.

"Good thing I have four bedrooms and no problem with a Falcone overtake. Drew, what about you and Peter and Mom and Dad? I can certainly make space."

Drew rolled his eyes. "You won't get our father out of his house, and he won't let his wife be anywhere but in his house. As far as Peter and, for that matter, Jimmy's twins, aren't they all at risk, with school? They could be snatched at any time, and you know, Peter is clueless to the family business, and Jimmy's boys are too young."

"We are overthinking this. We will all continue on as usual until we leave for our negotiation. Then we can decide the best course of action while we are away."

"We?" Dean asked?

"Yeah, Dean, you and me, we will need to go, as you will be the first to take both the Falcone and DeLuca families and bind them. You need to be there. Drew, Josh, and the rest of the crew will remain behind to help protect our loved ones."

The men finished their meeting, and Jimmy threw money down for Gorgi as usual and left the bar. He had kept most of his thoughts and reservations to himself. What needed to happen was going to be very dangerous and would necessitate excellent planning.

Jimmy drove down to his lawyers, and on the way, he called his father. When his father, James Sr., answered, Jimmy told him to call back on a burner. Less than a minute later, Jimmy's phone rang with an unknown number.

"Hey, Pops."

"Jimmy, what's going on? Is everyone okay?"

"I have a question for you. And I need an honest answer."

"Shoot."

"Did you know Al is not really a Carbone?"

There was dead silence on his father's end of the phone. Then he said, "Oh, Jimmy, that is surprising news. Congratulations. Let me get to my office, and I will get that number for you." He assumed his pops had company. Al's father?

"Jimmy, what the fuck? What the hell is his last name?" the old man asked a few minutes later.

"Siderna. We have both been had, Pops, by the world's fastest-growing Mafia Family. I think befriending us was part of the long game, or maybe it's a newer thing. Either way, we're in danger, and I want you to fly out here incognito, under your alternate identity. Does Alphonse know of that identity?"

"No, son, only you and Maria, bless her heart."

"Okay, I will keep you posted as to when. I have a lot to fill you in on, but once you arrive. I want it to look like you have flown home to Sicily, get the rumor mill going that you going to visit before the wedding here, capish?"

"Yeah, I get it, son, and Theresa and the kids, everyone okay?"

"Maggie was attacked in the woods but survived. As I said, shit is going down, and I need you here."

"I'll see you in twenty-four hours."

"Pops, please, be careful and secret. We'll wipe records of coming here and have Josh break into the airport data mainframe to make it look like you flew to Sicily. Purchase a ticket, and he will make it look like you arrive in Italy."

"I understand. Well, you say hi to everyone and can't wait for that wedding. Give my princess a kiss from her Nonno."

"I will, Pops, take care."

Jimmy hung up the phone and parked. It was time for part two of his plan.

Chapter 14

Maggie was on the lounger on the rooftop relaxing in the sunshine. The heat felt like a balm to her soul. Despite yesterday's events, she felt optimistic. After all, when one removed the darkness, there were many things to be happy about.

She was marrying the most awesome man she'd ever met, her childhood crush. She lived in a beautiful, enviable home. She loved her parents and her career choice. Life was good, and because of this, she reached out to Emma.

"Ems, it's Mags."

"Oh, hi. I didn't see your number pop up."

"Yeah, new phone. So I wanted to say hi, you know, catch up. How are you?"

"I'm good, enjoying the summer before school kicks in."

"Right, me too. That, and planning the wedding, you're still coming, right?" There was silence on the other end of the phone. "Ems, please tell me you are coming. Before our parents got in the way, we were besties."

"Your entire family will be there, Maggie, and I'm sure I

will get the cold shoulder. I just don't want any conflict in my life. Can you understand that?"

"I do, Ems, but you are doing your own thing, right? You're not working with your dad in business, so why would anyone give you the cold shoulder?"

"I don't know, guilty by association, I guess. Honestly, I have had to endure a few formal dinners, and they were a nightmare."

"Seriously? With the Marino Family?"

"Oh yeah, that horrible woman, Felicia, and that guy from school who used to like you, Damon, he was there too. I don't know what happened to that nice kid, but he is a stone-cold killer now."

"Wow, I haven't seen him since graduation. I didn't know he worked for your dad."

"Yeah, I usually never see the guy, but I did last week and was blown away by how different he was. My new name for him is Mr. Ice."

Maggie laughed.

"So, how are the wedding plans coming along?"

"To be honest, I haven't done much. Theresa and my father are the ultimate organizers, so they are doing most of it. I could use some help with my dress, though. Feel like taking a look? We are, after all, moving in the same fashion circles."

"I would love to see what you're working on."

"Great, how about Sunday? Come for dinner."

"But, Mags, I'm not allowed at your house, remember?"

"Oh, I'm not there. I'm at my new palace, with Dean."

"Shut up! Seriously?"

"Oh yeah, seriously, and wait until you see it!"

The girls moved into their old pattern of talking with each other like nothing had happened. Emma laughed at the story of the first night Maggie saw her new home. An hour passed in minutes for Maggie when she finally hung up the phone.

She couldn't wait to see Emma on Sunday and prayed that she would get the green light from Dean that Ems was safe and the girls could reignite their friendship for real.

Dean arrived home an hour later, to find Maggie dancing in the kitchen as she tried with her one good hand to make dinner.

"You're just on time, handsome, can you give me a hand?"

Dean dropped his laptop case on a kitchen chair and pulled Maggie into an embrace. She could feel him needing her, and she used her good arm to pull him tight to her.

"Are you okay, my Italian caveman?"

"Caveman?" Dean said, laughing. "Just because I'm infatuated with your gorgeous ass doesn't make me a caveman."

"Uhuh, and if I told you I had been chatting all day on Instagram with the hot guys who follow me, what would you do?"

Dean pressed her back so he could see her face. "You're pushing me, Bella, you know what I would do—mark your ass and then take it to show you I own you."

Maggie laughed. "Exactly, caveman. Now would you help me?"

"Of course, mia, let me change first and get out of this monkey suit." He disappeared and came back ten minutes later in shorts that hugged his hips and nothing else.

Maggie felt her walls clench at the sight of him. "Seriously, Dean? How am I supposed to finish making dinner with you looking like that?"

Dean imbued an innocent look and batted his eyes at her. "Well, I think it's fair, as you are wearing those tight shorts and a sports bra. All I want to do is lick you from top to bottom."

Maggie dropped to her knees in front of him, her eyes dilating as she peered up at him. "Me too," she husked and, using her good hand, pulled his shorts down over his taut hips.

His cock sprang out as she knew it would, and she took it in her mouth.

"Mm," Dean growled, "this is a great welcome home gift. Thank you, Tesoro."

"It's not for you," Maggie said, popping his cock out of her mouth. "It's for me, but I'm glad you like it too."

She flicked his tip with her tongue. Then she took his cock in her mouth, almost down to the root. Dean sucked in a breath as Maggie swallowed his cock for the first time. She'd been reading about how to do this and wanted to surprise him. By the sound of his reaction, she'd gotten that and more.

Dean started mumbling in Italian as he held her head gently, even in his ecstasy, mindful of her scalp that had been tugged so harshly by Damon the day before. She worked to keep her throat soft so as not to gag as she worked him. Dean was so turned on that he came seconds later, pumping his seed down her throat and turning Maggie on.

Although she didn't expect anything in response, she was drenched and hoped he would respond in kind. When he straightened, he gazed down at her. "That was the best I've ever had. Wow, I don't know what got into you, but I sure liked it." He pulled her to her feet and gifted her with a gaze that shot straight down to her core.

Moving her gently backward, Dean laid Maggie down on the table and lifted her heels to the edge of the table. He bent down and licked her from her sodden seam to her back hole. Maggie let out a guttural moan, arching her back wantonly.

He slid a finger into her ass and one into her weeping vagina, then began to work both ends in unison as he played her nub with his tongue. Within seconds, Maggie was begging to come, but he wouldn't let her until she was close to genuinely losing it, then when he said, "now," she let go, and a torrent drenched his hand and face.

Dean straightened, and Maggie could see he was hard

again. He could recover fast, and she was glad of it as she wanted him inside her. He turned her over and took her from behind, so hard and fast that she came without permission.

He pulled out and spanked her ass with a spatula that was within reach, and while he did so, he played with her hardened nub. She cried and begged to release again. The heat building in her nether region from the spatula was almost too much to take. Maggie became feral and screamed her need. When Dean said, "Now," again, Maggie came apart, her body writhing and spasming with pleasure, and it didn't stop. She felt herself in the grip of her orgasm for what seemed like minutes before her sensitive body finally relaxed.

"Wow, I think you went primal on me, Maggie."

"I think so too," she mumbled. Her legs were trembling with the effort of staying on her feet. "Please, can you help me to the couch? I don't think I can make it."

Dean swung her up into his arms and carried her to the big lounger sofa opposite the kitchen, so she could watch him finish cooking her dinner. He placed her down, then picked up her discarded shorts and went to their suite, grabbing pajama shorts and fresh undies for her. He cleaned her up and then helped her to put on the undies and shorts. Once settled, he grabbed her water and a glass of wine. By the time she drank some water, the trembling had stopped.

"Thank you. I don't know what's wrong, but I feel unable to control my limbs."

"I think you released more than your essence, Mags. That was a primitive release of your base nature. How do you feel now?

"Surprisingly renewed. Weak, like I just went through a transformation and came out a new person. So, do I look different?"

Dean chuckled. "No, you look well fucked, and I think that is my favorite look on you."

Maggie blushed as she watched him strut to the kitchen to finish making the dinner she had started. She felt surprisingly relaxed and comfortable as she watched her husband-to-be putter around the kitchen. She felt like she had as a young girl watching her father cook. Jimmy was an amateur gourmet chef, and Dean was proving to be talented in the kitchen too. But that made sense. His mother was an excellent cook.

"Dean, can I ask you something?"

"Sure, babe."

"Did your mother teach you to cook?"

"Actually, my mother shooed me out of the kitchen most of the time. She believed that only women cook and they should take care of their men and that one day I would marry a woman who did all the cooking."

"Seriously? Old fashioned much?"

"You've met my dad. Do you really think he would accept anything but?"

Maggie thought about that. Dean's dad had always been really nice to her. Too nice, but not so much with Dean's mom.

"Dean, was your father abusive to her or to you and your brothers?"

Dean handed her a plate and a fork.

She dug in and took a bite of the chicken and rolled her eyes with enthusiasm. "Oh my god, this is so good. Thank you."

"You're welcome. Now in answer to your question, other than the usual discipline stuff, no, my dad was never physically abusive. Being away and leaving us to be raised solely by my mother, was abusive. Their marriage was prearranged, and they get on fine, but they don't have a great love like us or your dad and T."

Dean wolfed down his dinner and took a big swig of white wine. "Now, let me ask you a question, cara mia. If we hadn't been told we would be getting married, do you think you would have ended up with Damon?"

Maggie frowned as she thought about that. "No, I think he might have taken my virginity, and maybe I would have thought he was *the one* for a bit. But his character never fit me, and I never admired him. I knew that I wanted to be with someone like my dad, someone I could rely on and look up to. Someone who could pick up the slack when I couldn't, a leader, and that man is you, Dean. You know I crushed on you big time when I was young."

"Yes, and I knew right away you were a spoiled princess."

Maggie flicked some water from her glass at him, and he laughed dismissively at her childish antics. "Dean, I have news. I spoke to Emma today, and it was the best! It was just like old times, and she is coming on Sunday."

Dean was not as enthusiastic as she'd hoped. "Does she know my bro is coming?"

Maggie squirmed. She hadn't mentioned Drew, but it hadn't been on purpose. She was just excited about the wedding stuff.

"Well, no. I asked her to help me with my wedding dress, to be honest. You know we are in the same fashion design school, right? Our little girl dreams had been to start our own label. I wanted her opinion of my dress, and with my arm like this, I also kinda need help."

Dean frowned. "You don't need help, Maggie. What is this about?"

Maggie dropped her eyes to her plate, no longer hungry, and set it down on the table next to her. "Nothing. Just with all the changes and the bad stuff going on, the wedding hasn't been discussed at all. I realized today that I haven't even talked about it with anyone for a while. Talking to Ems reminded me of my dress and, well, anyway. I'm re-energized and want to get going on the wedding."

He smiled at her. "I understand, and I'm glad you're excited, but we agreed, nothing until I've had a chance to meet with her and we get some more intel into her part in the family business."

Maggie smiled and nodded. "Yes, I totally understand. Did you get the chance to talk to Drew and find out what has been bothering him?"

"Did I. What a clusterfuck. Drew has been working for Damon since high school."

Maggie was shocked. "How? Why?"

"You'll laugh, even though it isn't actually funny. Drew has had a mad crush on Ems, as you know. Well, Damon told Drew that if he did errands for Al, then he would see Emma all the time."

Maggie was floored. "What an ass! Damon is so destructive."

"It gets better. Damon used Em as bait to get my brother out of the way. That is why it took him so long to realize that you and Damon were hanging out."

"Wow, even back then, he was a manipulative creep."

Dean nodded. "Apparently so."

"Can we go relax on the rooftop, watch the sunset?"

"Of course, we can, and I have the perfect accompaniment… tiramisu and dessert coffees. But not for you, bad girl, unless you finish your dinner."

Maggie looked at him, trying to decipher if he was serious.

Meanwhile, Dean's expression had grown severe and stern.

"What if I don't want to finish?"

"Then you will get sent to bed with no dessert."

"Dean! I'm not a child. You can't do that."

"Yes, I can. Now eat."

Maggie picked up her plate and finished her dinner. It wasn't a huge portion, and after she'd finished, she was confused as to why she'd made a fuss.

After they were settled on the rooftop, Dean answered her unasked question. "It's in your nature to push the boundaries, Mags. I know that, and it's fine with me. But I have the right to allow it or not. Understand?"

"What do I have the right to allow or not?"

"That's easy," Dean answered. "Anything you feel crosses your boundaries, you are free to bring up with me anytime."

"Really?"

"Truly."

Maggie felt better and relaxed back with her coffee and dessert, catching the last few rays of the sun before it disappeared for the night.

Chapter 15

"Maggie, when is Ems due to arrive?"

Maggie came out of the bathroom in nothing but her boy shorts and bra, giving Dean an instant hard-on.

"She's coming early, to go over the dress with me. About four pm, and I thought dinner at five-thirty? You're still barbequing?"

"I am. I was thinking chicken, lamb, salmon skewers, fresh bread with oil and balsamic dip, fruit, and grilled Caesar salad with baby prawns. What do you think, sound good?"

"I think, Maggie said as she sashayed over to Dean, "that it sounds almost perfect."

"Almost? What am I missing?"

Maggie dropped to her knees and yanked down Dean's shorts. "Hot dogs," she hissed and then took Dean in her mouth.

This woman would be the death of him, but if this was heaven, he would happily die right now. "Maggie," he growled. She moaned on his cock, sending a vibrational wave through him that had him almost spill. "You're so naughty, and I love that about you."

Maggie moaned again, and he was done for. Gripping the hair at the sides of her head, he pumped his seed down her throat. All the while, she gazed up at him, her big, innocent almond eyes gazing into his as she swallowed. Maggie Falcone was by far the hottest woman he had ever laid eyes on.

"Damn, woman," he said, helping her to stand. "That was amazing, Mags. How did you get so good at blow jobs if you never gave one before me?"

She smiled. "I told you about the vibrator? I practiced with it before our first time together. Then after when we had sex the first time, I watched a tutorial. I have been practicing at relaxing my throat, as you are considerably thicker than my vibrator."

"Maggie Falcone, you are full of surprises. Now, I need to get to the store. Is there anything you need, principessa?"

"Wine? Or have you thought of that already?"

"I have the pairings chosen for our meal, don't worry. You have begun your cycle. Do you need, uh, that stuff?"

Maggie couldn't stifle the laughter at Dean's discomfort. "I haven't been out of the house in days. Can I come with you?"

Dean frowned and then got sucked in by her puppy dog eyes pleading with him. "Yes, but we are taking extra security with us. And... you stay by my side the entire time. Understand."

Maggie nodded enthusiastically, and Dean helped her into a sundress that showed off her gorgeous coloring and smoking hot body. Then he texted Rael, who was heading up his extra security.

Maggie and Dean went down to the parking level and got in their SUV, checking to make sure that Rael and Steven were with them. Then they sped out and headed to the Italian market where Dean could find the fresh meat he wanted.

He hated having Maggie out in the open like this and prayed nothing would happen. He thought about the call he'd received from Jimmy the night before. Apparently, James Sr. was in town and would be attending the A2 meeting with him and Jimmy.

Things had been tranquil, and Dean wondered what was brewing. According to Jimmy, with whom he talked daily, no one knew where Damon DeMarco was. Dean rechecked his rear-view mirror and, seeing security was still tailing him, breathed a sigh of relief.

A moment later, he pulled into the lot and was glad to find it busy with life. If Damon was somehow planning to attack, he wouldn't risk a location with so many witnesses. Forty-five minutes later, the couple returned to their home.

Dean went straight to the kitchen to start prepping and then moved the prepared food to the rooftop and his pristine state-of-the-art outdoor kitchen. Maggie followed him around from one task to the other, looking for ways to help out. But with her arm, she was more in the way than anything else.

Dean had finally had enough when she almost knocked over the tray of chilled wine glasses he had selected for their food pairings. "Margaret Falcone, what has gotten into you?" Dean finally took a good look at his fiancée and saw that she was just barely keeping it together. "Maggie, Tesoro, what is bothering you?"

Maggie dropped her eyes as she fidgeted but didn't answer. The light dawned then, and he remembered something Jimmy had said. Glancing at the time, they had about forty minutes until Emma was due to show up.

Dean took Maggie's good hand and guided her downstairs. He took her into his walk-in closet and, pressing a button on the panel beside it, a wall swung open. Dean pulled himself and Maggie through into a space that held only one piece of furniture, a spanking bench. He watched her face for signs to show him what she wouldn't share verbally.

Her eyes went big, and then her pupils dilated. Despite her excitement, Maggie was stressed about seeing Emma. Without a word, Dean helped her onto the bench and strapped down her wrists and her ankles.

Maggie finally found her voice. "What are you going to do to me?" she asked in the sexiest voice Dean had ever heard come from her perfect mouth.

"I'm giving you a stress release, Bella. Now be quiet, or I will gag you."

Maggie relaxed, and Dean pulled a nice soft leather paddle from the built-in shelf hidden behind another panel. He brought it down on Maggie's behind at medium strength, loving the sound of the leather as it slapped her skin. It was a perfect implement for this moment, as it wouldn't leave a lasting impression. The leather paddle made a beautiful *thrump* sound as it landed on her bottom.

Fifteen minutes later, he put down the paddle and found Maggie deeply turned on, her beautiful cunt weeping for him. "I see you liked that, cara mia."

"Mm," was all she said.

Dean chuckled and pressed two fingers into her drenched folds. She barely moved but whimpered and mewled, carrying on until he told her she was free to release. With permission given, Maggie unleashed her wanton cries, turning into one extended keening release.

The sounds of her pleasure created an uncomfortable situation for Dean between his cock and his shorts. Yanking them down, he entered her in one swift motion.

She squealed with delight. "Yes, oh yes, fuck me, Dean. Harder, please… Ahh!" Maggie tipped off the edge, and Dean followed her, grunting and panting as he released for the second time that day.

He untied her and helped her to stand. "Better?"

"Much, thank you. I didn't know how to ask, and I wasn't even sure what I needed."

Dean grinned down at her and, moving a sweaty strand away from her eyes, he said, "You don't have to. That's what I'm for. Emma will be here in about fifteen minutes. You should go get cleaned up." He smacked her ass before she disappeared into the bathroom. Then he went to take his last load of food to the rooftop and came downstairs in time to catch Steven helping Emma from her car.

Dean remembered her from school, but she had changed a lot, and if he guessed correctly, he was looking at a woman who was rebelling against everything. Dean smiled at the knowledge, knowing if she ended up with his brother, that wouldn't last long.

He pushed all thoughts of Drew and Emma being together from his mind. Until Emma was cleared, this would be a friendly interrogation. Dean answered the door and was cordial to Maggie's ex-bestie.

"Hi, Dean, I brought wine."

"Wonderful, come in." He did the kiss on either cheek, a sign of family, and Emma stepped across the threshold.

"Wow, this is beautiful."

"Thank you. I know Maggie is excited about giving you the tour and showing you what she's been working on. Grab a seat, and I'll get you a drink."

Emma had just sat down on the barstool at the counter when Maggie came down the stairs, squealing with delight. "Emma!" She bounded over and awkwardly threw one arm around her friend.

Emma, a few inches shorter, wrapped her arms around Maggie's middle and returned the hug. "Hey, Maggikins, that looks painful, how are you holding up?"

Maggie pulled back. "Thanks, I'm good. Let me show you the house."

Both Emma and Dean were chuckling at Maggie's enthusiasm.

"Hang on, party girl, I'm making Ems a drink. What would you like, principessa?"

"Mmm, melon martini, please."

"Coming right up."

The girls chatted while Dean made the drinks and handed them over. "When you're ready, come up to the roof," he told them.

The girls giggled, and Dean was reminded of high school. How many times had he been passing by their lockers to find them exactly as they were now? "Okay," they said at the same time and broke out into peals of laughter as they walked off.

He shook his head in amusement. It was going to be a long evening. He wondered if he should warn Drew that Emma was here and then decided against it. If Dean had to suffer through their antics, then so would his brother.

An hour later, Steven alerted him that his brother had arrived, and he let him in. The girls were nowhere around, so he took his brother up to the roof for a quiet beer. Halfway through their third, Dean heard loud laughter as the ladies approached.

A grin split Dean's face as Drew's eyes narrowed at him. Maggie and Emma came stumbling out onto the rooftop, both in barely-there bikinis. Drew's eyes rounded as they rested on Emma, and then they narrowed in appreciatively.

Even Dean found it hard not to look at the two of them. The girls had been cheerleaders and led the squad together all through their high school years, competing both regionally and nationally. They both had great asses and sexy legs, but in bikinis, one could also appreciate the long, defined muscles and their pert, full-sized breasts. Dean had a dirty image play in his mind. He quickly shook it away.

Dean watched as Emma noticed Drew's presence. Her eyes grew wide, and then the little tart licked her lips. Drew was good-looking, a buff football player, but he wasn't as wide as Dean. In clothing, his brother looked like one of those Isnta models.

"Drew, how nice to see you," Emma said and then giggled. "You look excellent." She nudged Maggie, who had been mesmerized by the interaction.

Finding her voice, Maggie added, "Yeah, really good. Emma should pay you. Uh, that sounded bad. I mean, Emma should pay you for your services." Realizing how that had sounded a hundred times worse, the girls broke down into peals of laughter.

Drew and Dean smiled at them. When they finally stopped, Maggie clarified. "Emma is designing a men's line, and you're built perfectly for her sporty GQ look."

Dean grabbed Maggie and pulled her onto his lap. "What about me, cara mia? Am I perfect too?"

Maggie's pupils dilated. "Too perfect. The world couldn't handle Dean DeLuca." She leaned in, and Dean didn't disappoint, taking her mouth and owning it.

When they pulled apart, envious glances were leveled their way. Wanting a change in direction, Dean stood, placing his princess down carefully, and then handed each lady a water bottle. "Hydrate, and if you're good, I'll give you a glass of sangria." Dean had been joking and was surprised when both women did exactly what he said. With the four of them now in one place and calmed down, it was time for the *get to know you* part of the day that Dean hoped would reveal Emma's connections with her father or lack thereof.

"Emma, how is school? Getting excited about your last year?"

"Oh my god, yes! But it's been great, and I've met some super people. Honestly, my best acquaintances have come from school." That gave Dean a place to start.

"Oh? That's wonderful. Maggie hasn't introduced me to any of her school friends yet."

Emma laughed. "Well, it sounds like you two have been busy with other things." She laughed again. "I haven't been busy with anything but school, so those friends have been paramount to me, and I do love gay men. They make great besties."

Before Dean could ask anything about her friends, the two ladies went off on a tangent about Bobby and Josh, as Emma knew both. "Speaking of, did he do the décor? I love it!" Emma squealed.

Dean cut in, "He did, and all of it is with Mags in mind. I wanted a palace for my princess." Dean noticed Drew rolling his eyes. "And Bobby wanted to put his stamp of approval on it."

"How much did his stamp cost you, brother?"

"Too much to share with company." The foursome laughed.

"So what are your plans after school, Emma? Are you going to start a label like Maggie?"

For the first time since she arrived, Emma was quiet. "I honestly don't know what's going to happen. My pops recently brought up the idea of marriage between another Family and me. If I don't do what he asks, then I will be cut off, disinherited."

"That sucks." Maggie sat up, taking one of Emma's hands in hers.

"Do you know the Family?" She glanced at Drew as she answered Maggie's question. "No, some up and comer that my dad has been doing business with. But remember that asshole from school, Damon? I told you came to dinner about a week ago. It's someone in his Family."

"Really?" Drew asked. "A DeMarco?"

"No, yes, well, DeMarco is Damon's mother's last name. His father's last name is Siderna. What kind of friggin' name is Siderna anyway?"

Dean froze but kept his face neutral as he glanced at Drew. Very casually, he asked, "I thought you were a Siderna?"

"Me, are you kidding? I'm a Carbone, Dean, you know that."

"Right, right, I must have been thinking of someone else." Whatever else she may be, Emma Carbone was utterly unaware of her father's dealings. "Let's go to the table. You guys can keep me company while I cook."

Drew poured sangria, refilling the ladies' glasses every time they got close to being empty. By the time they got to eat, the ladies were pretty inebriated, and both tongues were wagging, unwittingly providing Drew and Dean with intel. The sun was setting as the group moved to dessert and coffee, and a lot more water. The ladies were considerably soberer after their large meal but sleepy. Dean suggested a swim, and the party moved down to the pool level.

Maggie had to be careful of her cast, but Emma and Drew wrestled and tossed each other around in the water. Dean hadn't seen his brother smile as much as he had this evening. And later, when the ladies went to shower and change, he suggested to Drew that they stay the night.

Drew seemed unsure until Emma came out of the change room in one of Dean's t-shirts and draped her arms around his neck. She planted a wanton kiss on his lips, and Drew pulled her in tight.

Maggie came around the corner next and stopped, a big grin lighting up her features. "We'll see you two later. Drew, you know where the guest room is."

Dean led Maggie out of the poolroom and up to their bedroom. Once he closed the door, he asked, "Did you manage to put the tracker on the phone as I instructed?"

"I did. Dean, what do you think about Ems?"

"There is more she is not sharing, but unless she is the best actress in the world, I'd say she is ignorant of her father's machinations for her future and his behind-the-scenes plans. She may know more than she realizes just because she still lives at home. Sometimes people say things that seem unimportant, but the brain stores them. I know of a technique to get the subconscious to unload. I did some tonight, but it is better without alcohol. If Emma is here in the morning, I will do it over breakfast. But ultimately, you have the green light to have her in your life. No going anywhere alone with her and no going to her house, capish?" Dean asked the last with a grin on his face, and Maggie giggled.

Doing her best Jimmy Falcone impersonation, she said, "Yeah, Dean, capish," her words coming out somewhere between Robert DeNiro as the godfather and her actual father. The two of them laughed until they were almost crying.

"Come on, princess, it is time to get some sleep."

The two climbed into bed, and Dean pulled her in tight, spooning her perfect ass against his crotch. The couple was asleep in seconds.

Chapter 16

Drew had been shocked when Emma stumbled out onto his brother's rooftop paradise. He had watched her hungrily all night and, when she spoke about her father's intentions for her, had growled in response. Thankfully, Dean was the only one who heard him and sent him a warning look.

Emma had been throwing herself at him all evening. When they wrestled in the pool, she had grabbed his junk and squeezed, with a very naughty glint in her eye. The evening wasn't late, maybe eleven pm, but for the two of them, the night was just beginning.

Emma sat primly on the edge of the king-sized bed in the basement guest room. Drew wanted as much space between them and his brother, who was two floors up. Dean's shirt was so oversized on Emma's 5'6" petite frame, it was hanging down to her knees. The neckline so broad, it sat on the tips of her shoulders. She looked like a little girl dressed in her father's clothes, her doll-like features adding to her younger-than-age appearance.

She put one delicate finger in her mouth as she gazed up

at him. She began to suck on it, giving Drew quite the show, but he was done with her performances. He'd been watching her all night, hell, his entire life. It was time for something more.

"Emma, you can stop. You already know I want you. I'm a sure thing, but I have conditions."

Emma popped her finger out of her mouth, her eyes rounded. "Conditions? Forget it, Drew DeLuca. I have those already, and I'm not interested in anything complicated. I just wanted a little fun." She stood and attempted to stride past him, but Drew wasn't putting up with her attitude.

He grabbed her arm and spun her back until she slammed into his chest. "Just listen."

"Fine," she huffed, blowing a loose strand of hair out of her eyes.

"I don't want a one-night stand with you, Emma. I have been in love with you since I was in kindergarten and you wore that cute pink romper to school on your first day of grade one."

Emma stared up at Drew in shock. "You remember what I wore the first day of school?"

"I do," he smiled, "and I also remember getting your lunch back from that bully Scott in the second grade."

Emma giggled. "You were so tall for your age that everyone thought you were Dean's *older* brother. At least until he sprouted up and got his adult body at fourteen."

Drew smiled. "Yeah, I remember for a short time I was his younger, bigger brother." The two giggled like school kids.

"Do you have other conditions, Drew?" Emma seemed very receptive now that she knew Drew wasn't interested in trying to control her.

"I do. You're mine, Dolcezza. If we have sex, there is no going back."

Emma's eyes rounded into giant orbs. "I, but what about my father? What do I tell him?"

"That you're free, my sweet piccolo l'uccello. Emma, do you trust me?"

"Well, yes, I always have."

"Then listen to me. I have made so much money running errands for your father and the Marino Family. I have a ton of money. Do you want a palace, like Maggie's? If you do, I will get you one. Do you want a company? If so, I will pay for one. You don't need to worry, cara mia."

"But, Drew, we've barely seen each other these past two years, and in school, we were only friends. How do I know this is the right thing for me?"

Drew, who had never been surer of anything in his life, said, "Let me show you." He pressed Emma back on the mattress and slowly slid her t-shirt up her body then bent down and reverently drew her legs apart, settling himself between them.

Emma was wet for him, her glistening entrance begging to be licked. He ran his tongue along her seam and felt her body tighten. Glancing up, he noticed her hands were gripping the bedspread. He kept his eyes on her body language as he flicked and played with her nub. She arched and cried out wantonly.

Drew forgot his sight and now used his sense of feeling to deliver pleasure. His tongue delved into her opening along with his index finger. Emma started bucking her hips. She was so sensitive and responded so readily that Drew was growing impatient to feel her warm, wet walls wrapped around his very hard cock.

Emma fell apart, squeezing his finger with her tight walls. Drew continued pumping, and within seconds, her second orgasm came hard and fast. She cried out with intensity, her entire body going rigid. But Drew wasn't done. He began to alternate between pumping her hard and then pulling out and playing with her hardened nub. It was almost a game, like turning the tap on and off, as she responded to him so readily. He had a hard time remembering what life had been before this moment with her.

Drew stood, stepping out of his shorts. He pulled Emma to the edge of the bed, and gazing into her eyes, he slid his length inside her tight sheath. Emma's eyes rolled back as she uttered a guttural moan and orgasmed again.

He couldn't believe his luck. His woman was so passionate, so responsive. He quietly thanked the gods that he was here with her. He took hold of her hips and drew her to him tightly. Then, angling down, he pumped her, hitting her cervix with his deep thrusts while she just seemed to orgasm, one after the other. Drew spilled his seed faster than he would have wanted but was proud he'd held out so long, considering how her walls had milked him like a pro.

They moved up the bed and under the covers. Drew pulled her in tight, spooning her delicate back against his much larger chest and loving how strong but fragile she felt in his arms. That was what had fascinated him all through school about the lovely girl. So delicate and so strong at the same time.

Now that she was his, he would worship her fragility, push her boundaries, and test her strength. Emma was asleep in moments, but not Drew. He lay awake for hours, making plans for his future, their future.

Chapter 17

J immy sat on the private bird with his father, future son-in-law, and four of his best security. Their flight to Ohio was an hour and forty five minutes, giving them plenty of time to solidify their presentation to the mob bosses.

Jimmy was surprised that all the bosses would be present. It would be the first time since the original Apalchin of 1957, which had turned out to be a disaster. But much had been learned from that fateful day. This time, only top commission Mafia Family heads would be there. That meant less than twenty men instead of one hundred.

Since the early 2000s, the mafia had grown better at covering its digital tracks and was no longer making rookie mistakes. Everyone was using an alias and flying or driving to the location, which was entirely off the grid and not frequented or owned by anyone in the mafia.

James Sr. had arranged for the old Catholic church, which was now owned by an animal activist group, to allow them to use the place for the weekend. It coincided with a relief group operation happening in New England, so the place was empty.

The mob bosses were under disguise as workmen coming in to renovate while the activist group was away.

The Five Families were the Genoveses, Gambinos, Luccheses, Bonannos, Colombos, then there were The Outfit from Chicago, and the Falcones. Jimmy's Family was unique because they had family in both The Outfit and the Five Families, descended from the Genovese Family on Jimmy's mother's side.

The Marinos were taking their orders from Sicily as part of the Gambino Family. Jimmy already knew that the Marinos were doing whatever the hell they liked, but that would end. He'd had John Gigliotti showing up on a different flight, to present the contract to the governing families. If they all signed it and agreed to the new structure, then the Marinos would be keeping their business to whatever Gambino decided. It certainly wouldn't conflict with Jimmy and Dean's spreading territories or legitimate pursuits.

It also meant that the families would come together to remove the Siderna threat at all costs. The families hadn't been a part of street warfare since the eighties, and they wouldn't this time either. Between them all, they had enough power to shut down every single revenue source the Sidernas had been encroaching on.

Jimmy had never been involved in the drug trade, weapons, or anything else. He'd been wholly engrossed in development through legal channels, with his most significant crimes being bribery and greasing politician's hands. Although, if he looked deeper into his intentions, one could say he was like the Bruce Wayne of Gotham, looking for ways to grow and stabilize the economy and business. Jimmy didn't get rich on others' backs. Jimmy got rich, and so did everyone he worked with.

He had become the man to work for, and he had helped to steer Dean in the same direction. Jimmy glanced at the man who was marrying his princess. He was deep in conversation with the elder Falcone, who was intensely listening to the younger man. Jimmy smiled to himself. He had picked a winner all those years ago, when he decided he wanted Dean to be a Falcone. The man was proving to be more than Jimmy could have hoped for.

When they arrived at the church, they were happy to see that everything was ready. Donating so much money to the environment group had its benefits. The place was set up like a café, and Jimmy knew the environment would suit the men who would begin to show up within the hour.

"Well, son, this is it. How are you feeling?"

"You know me, Pops, always ready for a show." Jimmy flashed his father his million-dollar smile. The elder Falcone grinned up at his tall son. "That you are, my boy. Has our friend arrived?"

"Yes, he is at the hotel with Dean and two of our security. The other two are hidden out in the bush, I would imagine, along with the others."

James Sr. laughed. "I'm sure you're right, bunch of paranoid bastards we are."

"For good reason, Pops."

The two men had just sat down with cups of strong coffee when the others began arriving. The Outfit's prior consigliere DeLaurentis, with his newly appointed second, Dom Gotti were the first. Although DeLaurentis was head, he was really just a figurehead of the old mafia's bygone era.

On their heels was the Bonnano Family head, Massimo Mancuso, and his son and consigliere, Michael Jr.. Jimmy, well acquainted with Jr., offered a welcoming smile.

Next, the Genovese Family, headed by Bellomo and his son and consigliere, Danny Bellomo, his father's cousins by marriage. The air was getting thick with strong aftershave and cigar smoke. Being a jock, this was one of the things Jimmy had always hated about *Family* gatherings.

He was busy talking to the Bellomos when the Gambinos arrived, John Gotti and his consigliere, Gene Gigliotti, cousin to the man he and his father were currently hiding at the hotel. Gene sent the men a look that said he knew his cousin, Jon Gigliotti, was in Ohio.

The Colombo Family was next, with their head, Russo, and his second, Mike Franzese. When the two walked through the door, aggressive energy came with them that always seemed to emanate from the Family.

They were just taking their seats when the reps for the Lucchese Family arrived. With their head in prison, Desantis and his son, Steven Jr. were running things. Nodding to the group, they took their seats.

When the room was calm, James Sr. stood up. "Welcome, American bosses and consigliere, to our A2 summit. It is my hope that this meeting proves fruitful to us all in the coming months and years and that we can form a bond that allows for more meetings of this type in the future."

Franzese addressed James Sr., "Don Falcone, why have you called this meeting? Your message said you had urgent business with the Five Families, but I see The Outfit is also represented. Why?"

"Thank you, Consigliere Franzese, for getting to the point. I will ask my son and consigliere, Jimmy Falcone, to explain, as he is the one who has made a discovery that affects us all and our livelihoods."

James Sr. winked at Jimmy as he sat down, and his son stood to address the room. "Gentlemen. I have been involved in recent disturbing events. As you know," he looked at Gotti and Gigliotti, "the Marino Family from Sicily made a move on us years ago. I dealt with that at the time by having a contract signed. I hold leverage over Joseph Marino's Family, and I also sold my legacy to keep the peace. What you don't know is that my right-hand man, Al Carbone, was in on the kidnapping and beating of my fiancée at the time. I left Al out of the negotiations, unpunished, as his father is my father's longest and dearest friend. But by doing so, I have left us all vulnerable, and I beg the forgiveness of you all."

There was grumbling around the room, and then Gigliotti spoke up. "You need to get to the point, Falcone, before we can offer you anything."

Jimmy nodded. Gigliotti was paving the way for Jimmy to share the rest of his tale. "Al Carbone is, in fact, Alphonse Siderna Jr. and has been hiding undercover as number two to Felicia Marino while conspiring to take down the Five Families and The Outfit."

The room was so quiet, you could hear a pin drop. Finally, Mancuso spoke. "Do you have proof?"

This is what Jimmy had been hoping for. "Gentlemen, I have proof of not only that, but of their actions. The Sidernas, or Kabalian, has infiltrated into our territories and expanded, not only without our permission, but also without our knowledge."

Jimmy reached into his briefcase and pulled out the organized stacks of packets he'd put together and distributed a set to each man. For the next three hours, the group pored over everything, from territories and deals that had systematically been removed from the families.

"Why haven't we seen this?" Russo shook his head. "Why aren't our capos keeping us informed?"

"My guess," Jimmy answered, "is either they are on the take, or, as we've seen, this plan has been laid out for the long game. A gun deal that went wrong or a drug deal that over several years has been decimated could be related to bad crops or increased border patrols. If they had done this all at once, you would have noticed. If you look, they are setting up all over Europe and Africa now. If we don't act immediately, we will be the losers, gentlemen."

"If we were all in agreement with you, Jimmy, and after all of this, it is hard to deny what you say, what then?" Danny Bellomo asked.

"I'm glad you asked, cousin. We form our own government, and once the positions are assigned and our underworld government is in place, we will sign documentation stating that anything done without our permission is an act of war."

"You have got to be kidding. If it was that easy, we would have done that years ago." The men in the room all grumbled in agreement.

"Would you have?" Jimmy Sr. stood up. "I mean no disrespect, but who would you have allowed to be the boss of the bosses? After the proposed idea in 1957, it never occurred, and not only that, but the aftermath was a business disaster. What my son is proposing is not impossible. In fact, it is very doable. The paperwork is already drawn up and awaiting your perusal. I suggest we take a lunch break and reconvene, ready to go over the new government plan."

Bellomo Sr. stood, by far, the most powerful man in the room. "I agree with James. I say we take lunch and then a look at what junior here is offering. All in favor say aye." Everyone agreed, and lunch was served while Jimmy found a quiet corner to call Dean.

"The group is ready to hear the proposal. Bring Jon down and come through the back."

"Okay, Jimmy, see you soon."

An hour later, Jimmy stood in the front of the space once more, this time with Dean on one side and Jon Gigliotti, his Family's lawyer, on the other. "Gentlemen, there has been a lot of information shared today that has made us question our role in business in this new age. To my right, is my future son-in-law and number two, Dean DeLuca, who was first to alert me to the real identity and the local mechanisms of the Siderna Family's plans. To my left, I'm sure many of you recognize Jon Gigliotti. Jon created the contract I needed to hold the Marino Family at bay and keep them from massacring the Falcone Family and empire."

Jimmy noted that Bellomo Sr. looked surprised and had at the mention of the Marino Family earlier. He had no doubt that steps would now be taken to determine what the Family was up to. "Jon is going to explain the idea of the contract, how it works, and answer any questions you gentlemen may have."

Jimmy and Dean sat down, and Jon took over, taking them over every detail of the three pages, outlining how this had come together and why it would work. Then the following two pages outlined their commitment and position within the new government. The Founding Family contract would allow all Family Heads, new and old, to play a level role in governing the outlined businesses included. Territories were newly divided and defined and worded to show the Siderna Family as hostile invaders.

When this was signed, and everyone was on the same page, the final stage of Jimmy's plan was next. "Gentlemen, I know you grow restless, but I have one more item of business. The Siderna Head and his number two, Al Siderna, are here to negotiate terms with us for their venture. As we are all now on the same page, they will be addressing us as the Founding Family committee, and we say what is allowed and what is not. Jon will be recording this meeting to ensure the Siderna Family remains honest in its dealings, which it hasn't so far. Are you ready?"

When everyone present had given consent, the doors were opened, and in walked Carmine, Al, and Damon. Jimmy wanted to be surprised that Damon was there, but he wasn't. After he met with Drew and Dean, Jimmy had gotten to work on his plan. The contract was only one part. He wanted to show the families what the Sidernas were really like, disrespectful, which the families would never support. Damon was the grandson of Carmine, the Head of the Family, and had been planted in Philly to take over from Al when the time came.

Beside him, Dean was ready to pounce. Jimmy, who was standing, placed one hand on his shoulder in a warning.

"Carmine Siderna, you stand before the reigning mafioso, accused of crimes against the Founding Fathers Committee. Crimes of robbery, the encroachment of our territories, extortion and theft. We would be in our right to have you executed on the spot. But as you have been given the benefit of the doubt, you may speak on your behalf."

"The found what, now? Have you fuckers made some shit up to try to take back what was taken from you? Good fucking luck." Carmine stood, smirking, along with Al and Damon. The three held a similarity between them that had been lost on Jimmy until they were all standing together. Jimmy waved his hand, and fifty guns pointed their way. The other Families knew Jimmy would be bringing in men, or they were informed once everyone was on the same page.

"The Founding Fathers Committee is a legitimate government, created to ensure that integrity is maintained in the mafioso. If you are negating its existence, then you are also negating your right to participate in it. Is that the case, Carmine Siderna?"

The don looked less sure of himself.

Al spoke up. "We haven't broken any rules, so why are we here?"

Jimmy felt gratified when laughter erupted in the room, and Al's cheeks turned a deep puce. Jon Gigliotti passed each of the three men a list of their charges and the proof of the transgressions.

Now the three changed from arrogant and flippant to desperate. "This means nothing." Carmine tossed his papers in the air.

"So then, you are choosing to negate the evidence? Carmine Siderna, you either sign the agreement that has been drawn up by our lawyer, Jon Gigliotti, or you will be judged and tried for your crimes against us." Jimmy wanted to rub his hands in glee. It had been years since he'd been actively part of the ruling Families. He'd been nervous at first, but he soon realized that being a gangster was ingrained from childhood.

"I'll sign," Al said and sat down at the table with a pen. The snake would live to see another day. Carmine and Damon, however, remained standing. Jimmy was about to pronounce the sentence when Damon pulled out a gun aimed directly at Jimmy Falcone. Dean managed to push Jimmy out of the way before he was shot and tackled Damon to the floor. Carmine also pulled out a gun and was wrestled to the ground by James Sr. Once both men were tied, the committee pronounced their decision. Carmine and Damon would be executed, and Al Carbone, aka, Siderna, was sentenced to leave the mafioso forever and retire to Florida upon pain of death.

The committee then moved to the back of the church and witnessed the two remaining Siderna men's execution. It was agreed that their heads would be sent to the Siderna Group as a warning, along with copies of the newly made committee.

When it was all said and done, the committee made a verbal agreement to meet quarterly. Jimmy Falcone was unanimously named the head of the committee and Dean DeLuca his second. The cleaners were brought in and the church emptied. Dean, James, and Jimmy were the only ones left.

"I can't believe what just happened," Jimmy uttered, dropping down into a chair. "Me either," Dean chimed in, "I feel like I was in a mafia movie."

James Sr. chuckled at the younger men. "Well, I, for one, am exhausted. What do you say, boys, should we go home?"

"Oh, hell yeah, I miss my Mags. I need to feel her after a day like today."

"Careful, lad, that is my granddaughter you're talking about."

Dean had been leaning his head back with his eyes closed. His head snapped up, and his eyes opened at James Sr. "I'm sorry, sir, I meant no disrespect, but it is true, I miss my princess."

James smiled. "I miss my queen and envy you, young man. You and Maggie have your entire lives ahead of you, and one day soon, Maggie will be your queen, and you will have a princess of your own."

Dean smiled at the old man. "I certainly hope so, sir."

"Come on, you two, let's get out of here," Jimmy broke in. "You're not the only ones wanting to feel a woman. I need T just as badly."

"Really, son, and here I thought things could have worked out between you and that Felicia woman."

Jimmy turned angry eyes on his father. Dean had seen what Jimmy had missed—a wink to say the old man was kidding around. At Jimmy's expression, the elder Falcone and the young DeLuca laughed.

Jimmy grinned. "I see Christmases are about to get interesting. I don't know if I want you two to get to know each other."

Dean and James laughed again at Jimmy's look of angst as they headed out the door for home.

Chapter 18

Four hours later, Maggie flew across the room and leapt into Dean's open arms. "I missed you," she said, peppering his face with kisses.

Dean smiled, loving her enthusiasm. "Have you been a good girl, Ms. Maggie?"

"Of course." She gulped. "Why wouldn't I?"

"Why? I thought it was obvious, Maggie girl. You know how much I love seeing my stripes on your perfect behind."

Maggie grinned mischievously. "Oh, in that case, I have been naughty, sir. I'm afraid that in thinking about you and longing for you, I played with myself and didn't even take pictures to send to you."

If she was telling the truth, then he would have to teach her a lesson, but for now, she was making up a game, a ruse to get a spanking. "In my office, little queen. For a lesson."

"Queen? No more princess?"

"No, Maggie, you were your dad's princess, the mob princess, but now, you're mine to train, mine to hold, and mine to love, and beside me, you are my queen, my equal."

Maggie's pupils dilated. "Oh, Dean, you know just what to say. How is it you know me so well?"

"You know, Maggie, for seven years, I have learned you and waited anxiously for you. I love you, Maggie mine."

"I love you too, Dean."

The End

Skylar West

Skylar West is a Canadian writer, new on the author scene and making a big impact with her steamy romance books. She loves walks in the rain, hot cups of delicious java, overly large sweaters, and the type of steamy sex she writes about in her novels. A cat lover, this author looks forward to writing many more novels.

Find her on Facebook: https://www.facebook.com/sky.west.1806

Don't miss these exciting titles by Skylar West and Blushing Books!

Sons of Sicily series
His to Learn
His to Train

Crown and Cross series
Laughlin

Angels and Demons Series
Fallen Angel
Dark Angel Discovered
Dark Angel Awakened
Dark Angel Rescued
Dark Angel Redeemed

Single Titles

The Dark Side of Kingsley

Anthologies
12 Naughty Days of Christmas 2020

Blushing Books

Blushing Books is the oldest eBook publisher on the web. We've been running websites that publish steamy romance and erotica since 1999, and we have been selling eBooks since 2003. We have free and promotional offerings that change weekly, so please do visit us at http://www.blushingbooks.com/free.

Blushing Books Newsletter

Please join the Blushing Books newsletter
to receive updates & special promotional offers.
You can also join by using your mobile phone:
Just text BLUSHING to 22828.

Every month, one new sign up via text messaging will receive
a $25.00 Amazon gift card, so sign up today!

www.ingramcontent.com/pod-product-compliance
Lightning Source LLC
Chambersburg PA
CBHW020647180626
46816CB00003B/1156